# RIM OF THE RIDGE

# Rim
## of the
## Ridge

Cena C. Draper

*Illustrated by* Emil Weiss

CRITERION BOOKS
*New York*

TO MY "MENFOLKS," MY HUSBAND AND SON

*And in memory of those who have passed along the winding banks of Postoak, Bearcreek, and Clearfork.*

# Contents

# RIM OF THE RIDGE

"Old Two-Toes is the spirit of the wilderness." said Hummy. "He's all the fine, careless, free things . . . he's Nature pitted against man, his gun, and his hunting dog. And I reckon there's nary a one of us who've trailed him that ever want to see him bested."

The boy knew he had learned one of Nature's secrets. In the plan of things, it was intended the biggest fish would get away, the fastest fox would outrun the hunters, and the smartest coon, like Old Two-Toes, would outtrick the hounds.

# ❊1❊

# *Rim of the Ridge*

Her shrill cry reached the boy's ears but he didn't stir. He heard her all right, but he wasn't answering. A fellow had to take a breather once in a while from nagging and everlasting Bible reading.

Let her keep on calling and see if he cared. Just let her wear herself out with fretting; it plain wasn't hurting anyone but herself. She could look till doomsday and she'd never find him in this hideout. Though he had to allow, she had a nose on her like a fox, his granny woman, and it tried his wits to outsmart her. For a fact now, she'd get wind of his tree house, no matter how cunning he'd been at building it.

Here he heaved a sigh as he looked about at his leafy roost. High as a crow's nest, it was, overlooking the rangy Ridgeland. It'd taken a heap of know-how, hoisting the hickory slats up into the tree and strapping them down snug. He'd sure been hamstrung on using a hammer, her ears being so keen. Most people when they got her age were deaf, but not Granny, no such luck for him.

No, he guessed he was about the unluckiest guy there was. To begin with, he didn't have any kinfolks in the whole world and a body sure hungered for his own folks. Course, there was the granny woman he lived with. But didn't he always remind himself she was just a stepgranny when he was clean put out with her, like he was now? Chances were that he'd understand her better or she'd understand him, if they were akin by blood.

Everybody around and near the Rim of the Ridge had scads of relations. Missourians were mighty clannish when it came to kinfolks. The hill people, living in Boone County, sure set a heap of store by their kindred.

But there weren't any Bunns any more; just seemed as if the family had died out, the same way the wild turkeys were thinning out.

Kind of a lonesome feeling it was, when at a church gathering or a basket dinner with everyone having their own kin. And who did he have? Or for that matter, what did he have? Did he have a single thing of his own, such as a dog? Such as a hound? Such as a hound pup? Bitterness welled up in him.

He looked at the date, 1902, that he had blazed on the tree trunk when he was twelve just four months ago. He'd had hopes then that the year was going to be different. But here is was more than half over and nary a plagued thing was changed.

"You, Punk, you!" The voice reached him again, unwearied.

There! Listen to the way she said his name. People called him Punk because his hair was a reddish color. But she said it almost the way you'd say . . . you'd say . . . skunk! That was it. Skunk! Oh, he was feeling sorry for himself. He guessed he needed a dose of Old Doc's liver tonic. Like as not he'd get a dose of it at bedtime about the time he got the Bible reading.

That Bible reading. Every day after every meal, he had to listen to the Old Testament. Listening to the words wasn't so bad. Their thunder and wrath made him think of the summer storms deep down in the timberland. Sometimes he even tingled to his very toes. No, it wasn't the reading he minded as much as it was their religion.

He groaned as he thought of the torment he was put through at school the beginning of each fall. Why couldn't they have been Baptists like 'most everyone else around the hills instead of being Dunkards? It sure set him apart, their manner of worship and gospel being so contrary to and unlike the rest.

Come to think of it, it wasn't the gospel part he minded, it was the way they dressed. Granny wore black with no beads or bangles, no pretties of any kind. She also wore a small, black bonnet. Seeing the contrast she made at the store among the other women of the Ridge went against the grain. The Ridge women wore bright calico dresses and hats with bits of ribbon and wreaths of flowers. A man liked to take some pride in the looks of his womenfolks (even of a stepgranny), but how could he, when she everlastingly put him in mind of a black crow.

Then there were his clothes to think about. He had a broad-brimmed hat and a suit of clothes with the unlikeliest pair of pants. Well, one thing he owed the Hood brothers, the hateful Toad and Spider, he didn't have to wear those pants to school anymore. Even Granny had to give up after they had shucked him out of his pants and sent him home without them about five times. He guessed he owed the Hood brothers plenty, but mostly it was another kind of owing. It was a debt he hoped to pay off some day. A debt of getting even . . . that's what it was. And no matter if that went against all the things Granny had taught him, he was bound and determined to have his revenge. He'd get even for all the meanness they'd panned out to him: making him eat mud, plaguing and heckling a fellow plumb out of his mind. And making fun of his granny, too. . . .

His thoughts came to a stop. He listened a second. What had happened to her? He couldn't hear her calling for him. She wasn't one to give up that easily. He began to worry. All kinds of things could happen to a heedless, hard-headed granny. It sure pushed a sizable piece of responsibility off on him, her being so foolhardy. Like now. He'd have to leave his tree house, dog take it, and find out if anything had happened to her. He sure was unlucky, for a fact.

He slid off the platform, working his way down onto a lower limb, and dropped himself to the ground. Chary, he decided to back-track and cover his trail like the big boar coon, Old Two-Toes, did. Wasn't anything smarter in the woods than a raccoon, Hummy Humphreys was forever telling him. And Hummy knew. He was the best coon hunter in the whole county of Boone.

The first thing to do was to find a trail that belonged to something else. And that is what Punk did. He squirmed himself along a narrow tunnel through buckbrush and weeds.

"Thank you, Br'er Rabbit, thank you, sir," he grinned to himself.

Then he came to the overflow stream from the big pond above. Bending low to escape any detection from the hill above, he stepped onto some stones in the stream and made a crossing.

On the other side, he made out he was going to slip off to the woods. It was all part of a strategy, as he was taking a new trail to go back up the hill. In coon hunting, this was called back-tracking.

All the time he was working to get himself up to the cabin, he was uneasily aware there wasn't a sound. The closer he got, the quieter it grew. Not even the scratching of a hoe could be heard.

He broke into a loping run and circled around the cabin. Not a soul was in sight. A fast run down to the hen house, a swift glance over toward the orchard, and a quick survey of the adjoining pasture revealed nothing. He made for the cabin and slowed himself down as he went through the back door. Wasn't any need to be all out of breath, as in all likelihood she'd be in her rocking chair or over by the wood stove.

He puckered his lips up into a careless whistle, circled the vacant kitchen, kicked the empty rocking chair, and brought himself up in astonishment by the big brass bed in the corner.

Granny was stretched out on the good counterpane with her clothes on, hands folded on her chest; her feet, in their laced black shoes, were turned heavenward. Her eyes were closed.

It fair chilled him to the very marrow of his bones,
Granny not being one to take a nap. Never once had he
seen her on top of the bed in her clothes either.

"Granny?" he ventured.

No reply came. But he was mighty relieved to see that
she was breathing regular even if she did look like she
was laid out proper for the grave. He cleared his throat
and tried again.

"Granny, what you doing in bed?"

This time he received an answer. But the words weren't
as comforting as he'd hoped they'd be.

"Taken to my bed to die, young man, that's what."

"You got a pain somewhere?"

A scornful sniff was his only answer. Bodily aches and
pains weren't to be tolerated.

It sure puzzled him. "You sick?"

"Heartsick."

Punk saw through it right away. She was trying a new
way to make him repent, he just bet. Well, it'd be a right
smart time, if ever, before he'd say he was sorry. Besides,
no one could lay themselves out on a bed and die just
because they had made up their mind to die. Of all the
unlikely things. . . .

"Knew a woman once"—the voice was hollow and weak
—"got it in her head to die and she just turned her face
to the wall and died." Granny sighed and slowly turned
her face away from the boy toward the wall.

Punk felt a mite uneasy, his granny woman being so
mule-stubborn. The cabin grew quieter while the Seth
Thomas clock seemed to tick louder and louder. It kind of
got on his nerves. He backed away from the bed and eased

himself down into the rocking chair by the fireplace. He
studied the figure before him. Was it possible, in willing
the spirit out of the body, a person could dwindle away?
He knew a snake could shuck his skin as smoothly as a
boy could take off his shirt. Maybe a mortal could do the
same. He began to feel kind of hollow in the pit of his
stomach.

"Granny...." He swallowed hard. No, dog take it if he
was going to give in.

Sensing his indecision, the woman let out a pitiful moan.
"Lord, lord, lord," she said, "a body gets powerful weary
of such a man-stubborn boy. Looks like it'll be up to You
from now on."

Punk slipped his hand down in his pants pocket and
fingered the leather band, the clasp, and the bit of metal
name plate. He didn't see how he was going to give it up.
Even though he didn't have a dog's neck to put it around,
he had the feeling of ownership just carrying around a dog
collar. Of course, it wasn't his, but he'd found it. Right
or wrong, he fancied it and he aimed to keep it. He clenched
his hand tight over it.

"If you go and die," he began fiercely, "I'll—I'll...." He
hunted about in his mind for something direful to stoke the
lagging Christian spirit. "I'll run off and join up with a
medicine show! And I'll get me a new store shirt and fancy
pants!"

The body on the bed stiffened.

"And—and I'll cavort with the Devil!"

She bolted upright on the bed.

"William Wallace Bunn"—her tone was measured—"the
Serpent is coiling himself about your soul. I daren't relax

my vigil one second." She was off the bed now, briskly smoothing down the counterpane. "Tonight you'll say the Lord's Prayer over ten times and. . . ."

A hullabaloo broke out back by the outside door, and Punk didn't hear what else she had in mind for him. There was a yelping and howling, deep-mouthed, that only hounds could make, and rising above it all in wrathful tones, a man's voice. "You dad-blame hound dogs! Cut it out! Let it go, consarn it!"

Punk made a wild dash for the back door. "Hummy! Hummy!" he yelled excitedly. He flung himself outside and right into the middle of three hound dogs and a tall, lean man who was kicking about with an irate foot.

"You, Blue! Melly! Red!" The three hounds, heads drooping, backed away from the man. On the ground was a chewed-up squirrel. Hummy looked at it a second and then directed a long look at the dogs. Punk saw it sure shamed them. Old Red had his tail tucked in between his legs, and Blue had fallen on his belly on the ground, while Melly just sagged in the middle like she was all done in. Hummy shook his head and made a low-tongue shaming sound. Then he turned his attention to the boy.

"Just happened to be passing by," he began, "with a fair mess of squirrels for Eliza Jane and golly Moses if I didn't go and drop one. These here crazy old hounds, so dern jealous of one another, near tore themselves in two. Been spoiling for a fight for quite a spell. Derned if I wouldn't give 'em away, if there'd be anyone fool enough to put up with 'em."

"You can stop that blasphemy, Hummy Humphreys, and dress them squirrels!" It was Granny, her usual tart self, standing in the doorway. "And you hound dogs, git! Kitchen floor all scrubbed up bright. I don't intend to have dog tracks all over it. Bad enough to have man tracks."

Right off, Hummy began wiping his shoes carefully on the grass. It never failed to dumfound Punk the way Hummy was always spooked by such a scrap of a woman.

"Well, now, Eliza Jane," Hummy's voice was very polite, "I can take these here squirrels on down to Widder Gregg's for supper. She ain't as particular about her floors as some folks I know."

"Not as particular about a lot of things, to my way of thinking," she gave crisp reply. "Weevils in her corn meal, ants in her sweets, clabber in her butter, flies in her milk. . . ."

"Whoa! Hold up there, Eliza!" Hummy was leaning against the door jamb with a slightly greenish look on his face. "I got me a queasy stomick."

Granny knew all about that weak stomach. Ever since the days Hummy had carried her schoolbooks down at Quail-Trap school, she'd known about it. It wasn't the first time she had used it to get the upper hand.

Punk noticed the pleased look at the corners of her mouth. He was some surprised how it changed her. It made her seem—well, less like a stepgranny. 'Course, he had to admit, she did have a nice face. And her skin was agreeable enough. Reckon if she didn't slick her hair back so tight she might not be so bad after all.

"You, Punk! Get the slack out of your pants! Rustle round and get the wood in for the stove. And you, Hummy, get them squirrels dressed. Sakes! The sun'll be dropping back of the hills and there'll be no vittles on the table."

Man and boy went at a half trot down below the wood-shed. The hounds, stretched in the shade of the elm tree, lifted their heads and watched closely. If the menfolks were leaving, they'd go; but if they were just stirring themselves, wasn't any need to move from the shade. An inbred keenness warned them to stay clear till their blunder was forgotten.

"Six squirrels!" shouted Punk as Hummy dumped them onto the ground from an old gunnysack. Wasn't anything better eating than fried squirrel.

"Had me seven," Hummy grouched. "Dern old hounds." He took a large clasp knife from his pocket, opened the blade, and set about skinning the game.

"Should have seen these fellers, Punk. I was down in the timber, way down below Clearfork yonder in that hickory grove, down to the old den tree. You know?"

Punk nodded his head. The den tree was one of the biggest elms in the timber, being there from the beginning of time. And way up, treetop, was a sizable knothole where the squirrels raised their families.

"Must have been a dozen or more of 'em, swinging off the grapevines and a-chasing one another around. A regular game of tag, it was. And the sunlight was streaking in through the leaves, spotting their red coats, and fuzzing out in sparks on their bushy tails." He paused and shook his head regretfully. "Sure hated to put my shot in 'em."

That was one of the things about Hummy that made Punk take to him. He sure had a real feeling for all living things. It didn't make him any the less man for it

either. Hummy was the best hunter, the best fighter, and
the bravest man in the whole countryside. Likewise, he
was the best dynamite man around. There was always a
job waiting for him in one or the other of the deep coal-
mine shafts there in the Ridge.

Way back, underground, the tunnels kept being pushed
further back to get at the coal. Hummy was the man for
the powder job. Whenever there was a risky bit to tackle,
it was Hummy who did it. Guess dynamite was risky, no
matter what. Men around in these parts had reason to know
and no one better than Punk. It had been dynamite together with coon hunting that had taken his pappy and
his grandpappy from him.

"You, Punk!" It was an outraged, briery voice from
the cabin.

"Fire in the hole!" shouted Hummy, a dynamite man's
cry when the fuse was lit and everybody better clear
out. Grinning, Punk raced into the woodshed gathering up
wood, and made a run for the back door. Doing chores was
fun when Hummy was around, and he didn't mind
Granny's sharpness either. Light-hearted, he stepped into
the kitchen and busied himself with the fire in the wood
stove.

Granny cast a swift glance at the boy's bright face, giving a deep sigh. But when she spoke to him, it was her
usual tart voice. "Things is still the same, Punk. Hummy's
coming is only putting off what you got to face. Nary
a second of peace will there be in this cabin till you make
things right."

"Well now, that shouldn't take a mite of doing." Hummy
was standing in the open doorway. His voice was steady

and direct. He stepped into the kitchen, bringing in the dressed squirrels and at the same time letting some drops of blood spatter onto the floor. Granny reached for her big dishpan and shoved it under the game.

"You menfolks," she scolded. "Out! Get out! Sakes! I'll do better here by myself."

Punk drew a breath of relief. He didn't want Hummy's good time ruined because of the feeling between him and Granny. Maybe the explaining could be put off till after his departure. Only it couldn't. Because as soon as they were outside seated by the well, Hummy said quietly, "Let's hear about it, son."

Punk squirmed. "Now?"

"Now."

Punk's hand slid reluctantly down into his pocket, bringing up the leather band with the name plate. He held it out to Hummy.

"Hummm." The man looked it over carefully. "Right nice piece of leather. Name plate, too. Name's gone from the plate, kind of rubbed out." He flashed a keen glance at the silent Punk. "'Course, brush and rock and weather, things like that, can wear a name off a soft piece of metal."

Punk gulped, making no reply.

Hummy's eyes watched a hawk set his wings as he drifted out over the woods beyond the cabin. Then he asked, "You found it, I reckon?"

"Down in the persimmon patch, Hummy, that's where I found it." Oh, he was eager to tell it to one who'd understand. "I was making a track through the thicket there, and I come across it. And when a body finds a thing, it belongs to him, don't it, Hummy, don't it?"

"Well, now, that depends. Depends on a couple of things, such as, say, no one claims it." He paused and kind of studied on it a bit. "And then if a feller makes a *honest* effort to search out its rightful owner, and nothing comes of it, why then it's his."

The silence kind of grew, turning Punk a bit queasy. He sure hoped it didn't last. But Hummy was a man of patience. He could outsit a buzzard in the tree. He could outwait a possum in a hollow log. It wore Punk down.

"Didn't you tell me once possession's nine-tenths of the law?"

"For a fact," agreed Hummy.

"And I sure got this collar in my possession, haven't I?"

"Well, now, I ain't so sure. If getting your hands on a thing makes it yours, seems like I got me a dog collar, it being in my possession." He was rubbing his thumb over the metal plate. "Funny thing, my thumb is sure spelling out something my eyes can't read. Yep, my thumb is sure tracing, J-u-d-d."

Punk knew right then how a treed coon must feel, because there was no gainsaying the fact he was treed.

"Toad Hood's got a hound dog named Judd, if I recollect rightly," Hummy was saying. "And this Toad, they say he's some scrapper, ornery mean. Might lay in wait for a boy that's smaller than he is some day and just might whip the living daylights out of him."

"I don't care!" Punk felt despair spuming up in him. "Oh Hummy, as long as I got me a dog collar, I can make out I got me a hound dog pup! Don't you see?"

Hummy put his hand on the boy's knee as if he were gentling a wild, scary colt. "No reason why you shouldn't have a dog collar, Punk, and if you'd told me, I'd seen you got one. But keeping something that ain't your own is all wrong, you know. 'Sides, you got a lot to live up to when you think about your grandpappy."

He recollected for a bit and then went on. "Old Billy Bunn. Wasn't afraid of nothing. Never backed down on nothing. And wasn't no one in these hills any sharper set on rightfulness."

Punk was sure shamed. It struck him as quick as summer lightning how mule-minded he'd been. Wanting to have his own way had plain made him lose sight of rightfulness.

"Well," he said, "I reckon it won't hurt none to ask Toad Hood if he's lost a dog collar."

"Reckon not," drawled Hummy, easy-like.

Right off, the boy began to feel better. He busied himself, lowering the pail down into the shaft for a good cool drink of water. The bucket hit the water's surface with a ping and went under. It took only a short spell to haul it up filled to the brim.

"Douse your face in that water and slick up your hair, son," called out Hummy. "You got to make peace with your granny woman."

Punk moaned. But Hummy didn't give him time to get out of it. He pushed the boy headfirst into the bucket and brought him out fast. A drying swipe of a shirt tail, a comb raked through the red hair, and Punk was ready.

As the man and boy approached the cabin, the smell of frying squirrel meat rushed to meet them and fair rocked them off their feet.

"Man, man!" exclaimed Hummy, clutching his stomach.

They stepped into the kitchen and took a quick look. A jenny wren couldn't have been any busier than Granny was: peeking into the oven, popping the lids on and off the skillets, whirling the spoon in the kettle of hominy on the back part of the stove, and jumping the large blue coffee pot around from one spot to another.

With a step as light as a girl's, she was moving back and forth between the stove and the round walnut table that was spread with a cloth. Only the man noticed her face all pinked up with heat and hair loosened into scoldy-locks.

The boy's eyes were on the table. Cracky, but it all looked good. Hungrily, he gazed at the dishes set out on the white cloth: the cottage cheese, the elderberry jelly, the newly churned butter and the green chow-chow relish. There was a crock of fresh milk with a big ladle beside it.

"Set," ordered Granny. "You two can have silent prayer whiles I make up the cream gravy and dish up the food."

Her lively, penetrating black eyes stared down the rebellious look of the two facing her.

"Silent prayer, I said. Ain't either of you so free from sin but what it'll better you to talk things over with the Lord."

Punk got a look at Hummy's startled face and he felt a big laugh coming up in his throat. It was Hummy's reply that saved him.

"Well now, Eliza Jane, t'won't be the first time I've held talk with the Old Man upstairs. He and me have been through some pretty tight spots together." Hummy's voice was easy and quiet-like as he continued. " 'Course,

I do my talking to Him out in the open under the skies. Seem to get closer to Him that way. And at night, when the darkness is all around, soft like a blanket, and way up overhead there's a light, like maybe the Door upstairs is ajar, why, then we talk. And you know, I got a feeling He likes it that way."

Granny just stood and looked at Hummy with point-blank bafflement. As for Punk, he had the best feeling. All of a sudden he knew he could talk to Hummy's Old Man upstairs and he could tell Him everything. He went straight away to his chair and seated himself.

But Hummy wasn't through. "You and me, Eliza, all these years, we been disagreeing with one another. Seems like we can't ever see eye to eye. It's always got to be your way. Now, I just got one question to ask you. Who's to say whose way is right?" He walked over to the table and seated himself.

"Might be, sometime, we find out our thinking's the same; we just go about it different." Hummy was as polite as could be as he finished with, "I'm not agin trying it your way." Forthwith, he bent his head and went into a deep silence.

Punk bowed his head and acknowledged to himself he'd do it his granny's way, too. Guess he'd take the dog collar back. Guess he'd 'fess up to the fact he'd rubbed the name off the plate. Guess . . . well, cracky, there wasn't nothing wrong in holding on to the idea of owning a hound dog pup of your own someday. When that time came, he'd buy his own dog collar, he just bet. He lifted his head and tackled his food with a cleansed soul and an eager stomach.

With supper over and the dishes washed (Hummy

scouring the skillets), they sat themselves around to visit.

Hummy stretched out by the hearth with his shotgun and set himself to clean it. Punk busied himself with weaving the cane bottom for a chair. Granny pulled out the ragbag and began braiding long strips of cloth which were going into a rag rug.

The light from the kerosene lamp threw out a round circle that held the three of them as cozily as the rabbit's burrow held its young. It was right comforting to the boy. Maybe now they could have some man talk, say, like hunting talk. Nothing in the world he fancied better than that. And Hummy could tell tales that were scarier than the big hoot owls in the timber. His descriptions were so keen and lively that oftentimes the boy felt himself running with the pack of hound dogs. Sometimes he was the hunted: the fox, winded and spent; the coon trapped in the tree; the wild turkey, wing-crippled. Those nights he didn't sleep so well.

What he liked best to listen to were yarns about Old Two-Toes, the big boar coon, the great grandpappy of 'em all! He was the scrappingest, schemingest, knowingest old booger of the woods. He'd been outfiguring the hunters for years. Once, when he was young, he had been trapped, as his name plainly showed. But t'wasn't likely it'd happen again. And Punk sure hoped it didn't. Like as not, deep down in Hummy's heart, there was the same hope: though he and his hounds were always giving chase.

"Have you heard the latest on Old Two-Toes?" Hummy asked, just as if he could read a boy's mind.

He held his gun up to the light and peered into the gun barrel to be sure there was no burnt powder there.

"He's sure in bad trouble this time," he continued.

"What's he done?"

"Drowned that pesty, surly hound pup of Toad Hood's, that's what he's gone and done!"

Even Granny shook her head over that. Wasn't a meaner, grudge-carrying family about than the Hoods. They'd sure be out to get Old Two-Toes now; even though the whole fracas had been their doing.

"It was self-preservation," Hummy nodded to the boy. "It was either kill or be killed and Old Two-Toes was bound to save hisself."

"I was in the timber down by Horseshoe Lake, heading for home," he began his story, "when I come on to the Hood boys and their hounds. I'd been hearing them for quite a spell. Knowed the hounds had a hot trail by the way their voices was coming in."

"And then I seen it happen. Old Two-Toes sprang from the trail and went swimming out into the water. 'Course, the older hounds had sense enough to stay on land. But that pesty young dog they been a-training was sure panting for the kill. Never seen a dog so set on killing. Out he sprung into the lake. And that coon, he rose up in the water and, quick as a flash, he climbed on that cur's back.

"There was all of us, shouting and yelling on land for that fool dog to come back. The Hoods were a-swearing plenty. But they weren't getting themselves wet in that water, feeling the way they do about water."

Punk snorted. The only time or place he ever had an advantage over the Hood brothers was in the water. They couldn't swim and they were plain scared of water. Many's the time he made his getaway by a quick dive into the lake. That old coon was sure smart, heading for the water the way he did.

Hummy went on. "They kept sicking that ugly old Judd dog to go in after the young one. But he wasn't having any part of it. He just dug his toes into the dirt and howled and howled. And all the time, Old Two-Toes was a-holding that whelp's head under water."

"Land's sakes!" Granny was on the edge of her chair, carried away by the tale. Punk got a real kick out of that, her being so set against running and trailing with hound dogs. Here she was as kindled up as he was about Hummy's story, as if she were his blood kin. But he didn't have time to think about that as Hummy was finishing his story.

"T'wasn't more than a minute till the thrashing and the churning out in the water stopped. That big boar coon rose up on the surface and, calm as you please, he turns and swims to the other side. He heads for Coon Rock and safety."

"Cracky," Punk let out a sigh.

"Them Hoods!" Hummy wound up. "Done me good to see them outsmarted. Oh, they had plenty to say, tromping about and swearing how they'd get even. But say what they pleased, they knowed the laugh was on them."

Hummy cast a look at Punk, who was worrying over the fact the Hoods had sworn vengeance on Old Two-Toes.

"Cheer up, Punk," Hummy laughed. "Them Hoods always been thick-headed. I'm wagering that old coon is 'way smarter than the whole caboodle of them."

Punk's hands resumed their cane weaving but his thoughts were out in the timber. It had always been sport to give chase to such an old fighter as Two-Toes, but he knew it wouldn't be sport that drove Toad Hood to look for the coon now. It'd be hate and spitefulness.

"How are things with you, Eliza?" queried Hummy after a while.

Granny looked kind of bothered. She didn't make reply right off. Her fingers flew on with the braiding of the rags. Suddenly, she put her work down in her lap.

"May as well come right out with it. May as well eat crow right here and now." She sat stiff and straight in her rocker. "Took it into my head to die about midafternoon. Stretched myself out on my good counterpane and made up my mind to die."

"That so?" Hummy didn't seem the least startled.

That was one of the things Punk admired about Hummy. Nothing could upset him. Why, not even catching his coattails on fire had disturbed him that time they were together in the timber.

"Coattail's afire!" someone had yelled.

"That so?" Hummy had answered, as calm as could be. Then he set himself right down onto the coat and flame and squirmed out the fire on the ground. Never was another man like him, the boy bet.

"Plain shirking my responsibilities, I was," Granny went on.

"Can't see as there's any harm done."

"The harm done was that I was trying to trick Punk into saying he was sorry for something."

"And it didn't pan out the way you'd planned it." The man cast a quick look at her. "Always have to have your own way, don't you, Eliza? Reckon no one knows that better than me."

Punk knew he had to act quick if he was to save the evening. If Granny got riled, she'd send Hummy packing and it might be weeks before he stopped by again. Now was the time to make his peace with her. He reached for the dog collar and, stretching across the short space between them, dropped it into her lap.

"Granny, the collar belongs to Toad Hood and his dog, Judd. I'm aiming to give it back tomorrow." He took a deep breath and plunged on. "I rubbed the name out. I was aiming to make it mine."

"Oh, Punk!" Triumphant, her voice rang out. "You've told the truth and shamed the devil!" She reached out and grabbed him to her. Then, as abruptly, she put him from her. "That don't get you out of saying the Lord's Prayer ten times tonight."

"No'm."

Realizing he'd have to give up the dog collar, sadness crept in on him. He sat possum quiet and brooded. A cough shook his thin shoulders.

"You, Punk!" Granny's voice was sharp. "Get yourself right up into bed this second. I'm fixing to rub your chest with some goose oil." She turned to Hummy. "Plain worrisome, that cough. He don't seem to throw it off. Now, if I had me some of Old Doc's tonic, I'd best that hack of his."

"Tonic?" The man was real thoughtful. "Come to think of it, I've got a tonic for the boy, Eliza, a real tonic. Might do him a heap of good."

Granny looked mistrustfully at him for a second. "Never knew of you taking up with any kind of a tonic, Hummy Humphreys." She turned back to the boy. "Now, then, Punk, the goose grease and off to bed."

He was greased and in no time bedded down on his pallet up in the loft. The boy was especially fond of his sleeping quarters. Long ago it had been used as a storing place for onions and dried apples, with their lingering traces haunting the loft agreeably.

Wooden planks had been laid down on top of the rafters. It was enough space for a pallet, a boy, and his dreams. The cracks between the planks let up flickering bits of light from the lamp below. Sparking against the sloping roof, they put him in mind of the fireflies that lit the hollows on warm, murky nights. And being in his loft was about the same as being in the room below, since their voices drifted up to him just as smoke swirled upward.

It was pleasuring to hear them until suddenly he was aware of a change of pace in the voices. It was plain the talk had turned quarrelsome. Now, he just bet Granny was riled and Hummy would be leaving. But no, Hummy wasn't leaving!

"If I set here clear till kingdom come, Eliza, I'm a-going to make you see this thing my way!"

"Set then! 'Cause that's exactly how long you'll have to set, Hummy Humphreys! Till kingdom come! I'm not about to let that boy go traipsing about the timber with you, a-running after a hound pack, chasing about the countryside!"

Punk's heart gave a startled leap. Hummy was asking for him to go with him someplace. And what's more he was putting up a fight. The boy lay very still and listened.

"You want to cure him of what ails him, don't you?"

"Running wild with you won't cure him of his hack, won't be putting flesh on his bones."

"And I'm saying it will! The boy's eating his heart out."

"For what?"

"For things you've long closed your mind to, Eliza." His voice was sad.

"You'll not be the one to be setting in judgment of me when the time comes!"

"No, I won't be. And I'm mighty thankful for that."

"Why, Hummy," her voice cracked in surprise, "in all our years, why, from birthing—fifty-three years—don't reckon we ever had hard feelings."

There was no reply from the man. And finally it was her voice that reached Punk's ears.

"A-setting yourself against me. Never figured on that."

"It's the boy we got to think about, Eliza. Time's long gone when we thought about one another." He cleared his throat. "Things is all wrong here in this cabin, the two of you pulling against one another. It's been coming on for quite a spell. I seen it coming. And now, I say give the boy over to me for a spell. I'll bring him back to you so that things will be right between you."

"A-fixing to work a miracle, Hummy?"

"Might be."

Punk drew in his breath. If Hummy got his way, it'd be nothing short of a miracle.

"And just how do you scheme to work this here miracle?"

Hummy was ready for her. "Ain't it the Bible that says there's a time for everything? A time for sorrow and a time for joy? Comes a time, Eliza, when a boy must have his way. The Lord intended it so."

"Humph." Granny was listening, though it was clear she was doubtful.

As creek water rises during spring rains, so Hummy's words began to flow. They were words that had been dammed up in him for some time now.

"A boy must run wild with the winds, his feet must touch the earth, his eyes must reach the sky. He must swing from the oak trees and grapevines, take the earth in his hands, baptize himself in the creek water.

"He must fill himself with the song of the birds and the streams, with the beauty of the night, its stars and moon and Milky Way."

Punk marveled as the words reached up and washed over him.

"You can't halter-tie a boy, Eliza. The time comes when he gets that hungering in him. Then he's the fox in the brush . . . he's the hawk on wing . . . he's the deer in the wild meadow. Comes that time, whether or not, and nothing can hold him back. Nothing. . . ."

Punk turned his face into the pillow.

As quiet as the fox in the brush, as swift as the hawk on wing, as stealthily as the deer in the wild meadow, sleep came.

## 2

# Past Horseshoe Lake

It was a long walk to the Hoods' shanty. But Punk didn't feel called upon to complain. The longer the walk, the longer putting off; the longer putting off, the longer he'd be in one piece.

He sure wished he'd let that piece of leather lay right there in that persimmon patch and rot. Because there was no shucking the fact that Toad Hood was exactly what Hummy had called him—ornery mean. There'd have to be a tall lot of explaining over that plagued dog collar.

Well, right now, he'd think about the distance and the spare time he'd have. Granny wouldn't expect him home till dusk. He could crop the time in half by the short cuts he knew to take. And he'd have extra time in the timber. Well, that old dog collar was good for something besides trouble.

A fellow's nose was kept to the grindstone with studying and going to school or doing chores about the place. Never seemed to be any time to fritter away, like a boy had a hankering after.

Not that he was against learning. Why, his whole heart and mind craved to be knowing more about everything. But school was just reading, writing, and arithmetic. The knowledge he yearned for didn't seem to be in the school-books they studied down at Quail-Trap. And the teacher couldn't answer any of the questions that continually rose up in him and pestered him. Questions like where did the birds go that left the Ridgeland; the wild canaries, the orioles, the robins, the rose-breasted grosbeak? And how did the woodcock make that whistling noise, with his throat or with his wing? When a hound dog hit a trail, how did he know which way to go? How did he? Why did the ground hog hibernate? Why didn't the cottontail do likewise? And how did a possum's babies get in her pouch? Were they born there? Oh, he had hundreds of unanswered questions in his heart.

Hummy knew a lot of the answers.

"Golly Moses, Hummy, will I ever know as much as you?" he had burst out one day after Hummy had been telling how a wood duck hatched her eggs and then carried her young down to the water.

Hummy had laughed. "It's right possible, son, right possible."

"How can I?"

"By using this" —he pointed to his ear— "and by using this." He touched his head—"and by using these"—he made a motion toward his eyes. "Wherever you are, just stop, look, and listen and use your head. Never enter the timber without stopping, looking, and listening. It'll be mighty rewarding."

Punk always remembered that. And it had been rewarding. He'd seen the courtship of a bobwhite and his mate, the hopeful strutting of the cock, the coyness of the hen. And later, he'd seen the mother quail leading her young through the brush, the young like bits of thistledown. He'd watched a fox and her babies playing with one another, rolling and romping. He'd observed a mother skunk conducting her children on a forage for food. He'd discovered that a coon's eyes glowed green gold at night and that a possum's eyes turned ruby red.

Golly, the many things he'd seen; turtles riding logs downstream, minnows a-swim in the creek, bass churning up out of the water, and beavers at play on a bank slide.

Through Hummy he had learned to read the adventures told by the markings on the ground, same as reading letters on a printed page. And a fellow didn't need the alphabet for that. Down at Horseshoe Lake, there were always exciting stories if one knew how to make out the tracks.

He could distinguish between the footprints of the fox, the coon, the rabbit, the wolf, and the bobcat. He noticed what they ate. If a fight had taken place, he could tell by the imprints.

He moved on slowly and quietly through the woods. The underbrush was deep, with paths made by the tenants of the woodland to take and follow. Light of foot, light of heart, he began the game he favored in the timber. He was Old Two-Toes, and close at his heels were the hound dogs. How to outwit them now, how to escape?

He began his maneuverings. First, he led the pack along a cottontail's route, twisting and turning through a briery patch. At a clearing, he commenced the tapping of the big trees. Running swiftly, he leaped up several feet on the side of the tree trunk, making contact bodily with the tree, and, dropping down, went on. Often such a trick led a dog to believe the coon was treed.

Coming to the stream, he followed it a long way, hopping from stone to stone. He noticed each growing thing. There was water cress growing at the water's edge. Occasionally, he took some of this home to Granny for her cooking. He paused and nibbled a sprig of it, rather savoring the bitey taste. Then he was on his way, crisscrossing and back-tracking along the waterway. By such devious routes, he brought himself to the place he had in mind all the time: Horseshoe Lake and Coon Rock.

Of all the spots around, this was his very favorite. At an early age, Hummy had taught Punk to swim. He was familiar with every twist and turn of the banks. He knew the depth of the water, where the sand shoals were, where the deeper places lay. He had explored every inch of the place. He knew how to dive under the moss, how to lie face down in the wild lily pads, how to hide in the cattails. He knew where the beavers' homes were and how they built their channels and tunnels.

There was something else he knew, something he'd never even told Hummy. It was a secret—a secret about Coon Rock.

Coon Rock was a huge, slick boulder that rose up from the edge of the lake. It reached up into the meadow and wild hay land: a jutting piece of rock, moss-green in color.

Above, from the hills that sat one on top of the other, were the ponds. During the rainy season and in the spring, torrents of water spilled from these inlets and ran in rippling cascades through the hollow. Finally, it spread into a waterfall over the edge of Coon Rock, ending in Horseshoe Lake. And where the water filled the lake was a foam like Granny's wash suds, floating lazily on the surface.

The boy had long considered the Rock as a challenge. And one day when no one was near, he had set himself a task. He would climb the Rock and go up as a salmon did in the cold waters of the North. And finding precarious footholds, he had climbed up the face of the boulder. It was then he had found his secret.

Up more than halfway, he had discovered a small opening. He had teetered there, fearful of what might be behind the gap, yet curious as a young coon. At last, plain bedeviled into it by his inquisitiveness, he had slid his body in through the cleft, finding himself in a cave. It had been downright fearsome at first, standing in the darkness, waiting for his eyes to grow accustomed to the gloom. There had been a sighing sound and a spookinesss about, as if it were a ghost haunt. But soon he had discovered the sighing sound came from a crevice overhead that not only let in bits of light but flurries of air. The cave was small but large enough to make a hideout. And the hanging moss and trickling water screened the entrance from human eye.

It was the one thing that belonged to the boy. Not even to Hummy, his best friend, had he ever disclosed this knowledge. He had found it gratifying having something of his own, even though it wasn't puppy-warm and wig-gling.

He wished he had time for a visit today, but he reckoned he'd better not. There were too many things weighing on his mind to take time off now. He had only to measure the sun with his eyes to realize he'd already dallied more than he should. It would be best to skedaddle on and get that collar returned to Toad.

Maybe, it just might be, Toad would be gone from the place and Ma Hood would be there. Punk hoped this would be so. Ma Hood was as good-natured and friendly as Toad was mean and ornery. Full-bosomed, lazy, and lap-fat, she never raised her voice to her menfolks.

"Now, Toad, hon," she'd rebuke her oldest, "I wouldn't have gone and done that if I been you. I sure wouldn't have."

Nothing riled her. Nothing pleasured her. Her life went along on an even keel. She made heavy sugar dough-nuts and yeast rolls, mighty filling to a hungry boy. And there was no stinginess on the sugar. Punk speeded up his feet. It was highly likely that Toad would be gone. He'd relish a visit with Ma Hood and her heavy doughnuts. He sure would.

He came out of the timber briskly and set his feet along the sandy road, fetching himself up at the Hoods' shanty in no time at all. Cracky. His heart sank, he was still the unluckiest boy on the Ridgeland. There was that skinny hound dog, Judd, and stretched out beside him was that no-good Toad Hood.

He pushed his lagging feet on up the road, then stopped in front of Toad. Judd was already on his feet growling.

Funny thing about hound dogs, Punk had noticed. They were like the ground lizards that took on the same color of their surroundings. It's said you can about reckon the nature and frame of a fellow by his animals. Now for instance, nobody would find sweeter, better-mannered hound dogs that Hummy's. Why, Melly was the sweetest hound ever to tree a coon. And Old Red and Old Blue never picked a fight, although they didn't back down on one either. They had the dignity and calmness of their master. They trod with a majestic gait, carrying their tails high and proud.

But take this hound dog, Judd. Nowhere in all the Ridgeland could one find a meaner dog: a lean, ribboned, tail-tucking, slinking bit of flesh. It plain revolted the eye to look upon him. He was the kind that would sink his teeth into a boy when his back was turned.

With Punk's approach, the dog was all hackles and throat-rumbling menace. The boy felt himself breaking out into a cold sweat as Toad rolled over onto his feet and faced him.

"B'jiggered!" leered the Hood good-for-nothing. "Look who's hyar! As I live and breathe, hyar is li'l ole Bunny Rabbit. Howdy, Bunny."

Punk managed a grin. "Hello, Toad."

Toad narrowed his eyes. Heck, wasn't he going to get a rise out of this skinny piece of flesh and bones? And what business did he have coming to this shanty and saying friendly-like, "Hello, Toad."

"Whar's them pants with the back door?" he asked. Seeing the flush steal up on the boy's face pleasured him and he let out a whoop and rolled himself on the ground.

Punk kept his hand down in his pocket holding tight

to the dog collar. He let the clasp bite into his flesh. It
helped steady him. He couldn't honestly blame Toad for
making fun of those pants. They had no pockets and they
unbuttoned on the sides more like girls' underclothes than
boys' proper wear. But he didn't aim to let Toad see how
bothersome he found his mockery to be. Just so he didn't
say that rhyme about Granny and her bonnet and her black
skirt, he'd be able to keep hold of himself.

"Oh, horse feathers! I jes recollect." Toad was on his
feet standing so close that Punk could see the wart that
hung to the side of his nose. "Them pants is yore prayer-
go-to-meeting ones, now, ain't they?" He pulled his lips
back off his teeth. "And that being the case, you Billy Bunn-
bunny rabbit, you should have wore 'em today! Yes sirree,
you sure should have. It jes might be we'uns will hold a
prayer meeting of our own, right hyar." He sucked in
on his yellow teeth with relish.

"Seems to me, I tol' you to keep away from hyar. 'Pears
to me you come along jes to stir up trouble." Toad shook
his head regretfully as if it were the last thing in the world
he wanted, trouble with such a nice fellow as Punk was.

"I came to bring you something," said Punk.

"Why, Brother Bunn, turning the t'other cheek, now?
Wal, that's considerable friendly of you, considerable
friendly I'd say." The mouth stretched wider over the
teeth.

"It's Judd's collar. I found it down in the persimmon
patch." He brought his hand up out of his pocket holding
the collar out to Toad.

Toad snatched the leather band from his hand. At this
sudden movement, Punk felt Judd move in closer. He felt

the wet nose against the back of his leg, the grumbling cold breath raising goose pimples on his skin. All that Hood monster had to do was to say, "Sick him!" and Judd would have a hold of his shank bone.

"Hey, Spider," yelled Toad abruptly.

There was a rustling, sliding sound in the tree limb overhead. No other sound. Spider was in the tree. He was never far from his brother. It was a familiar sight to see Toad Hood around with Spider following at his heels, moving with a queer, crablike gait, moving silently. Spider had been born dumb. It was downright scary to come up on him without warning. The pallor of his face, together with his colorless eyebrows and hair, gave him a look of ghosts and dead men. The beady small eyes that watched and yet shifted away from any direct look were frightening, too. Not that he ever did any harm. It was Toad who did the fighting. Spider only sat and waited. But it was the waiting that got on a fellow's nerves. He'd seen the timber spider in his woven web just so attentive when he ogled a victim.

"Hey, Spider, look at this! Here's that old Judd dog's collar, plate and all!"

The swish of the leaves indicated that Spider was looking.

"B'jig-jig-jiggered!" Toad looked curiously at Punk, trying to figure out a fellow who'd return a collar that had a valuable silver plate.

As for Punk, he knew then he could turn and make a clean getaway. He could take himself off without the possiblity of Judd attacking him or that Hood ruffian beating him to a pulp. Run, go on, run, his common sense kept urging him. But something else held his feet planted as firmly in the dirt as if he were a carrot, root deep in the garden. He was sure in for it, if he said another word. The minute he confessed to rubbing out the name he was a dead duck. But he promised Granny he'd make a clean breast of it and if there was anything he set a great store by, it was telling the truth.

Punk just squared himself about and blurted out, "I was of a mind to keep it." The words were louder than he had intended and they sounded brash and quarrelsome to his ears. But he kept on plowing his way through his confession as doggedly as when his plowshare hit rock and dragged. "I went so far as to rub out the name to make it mine."

Toad stood open-mouthed. Not a sound came from the tree. Even Judd laid off his muttering. Punk had the feeling that his words had bidden the very earth to stand still, the wind to stop blowing, the grass to cease rustling. His feeling of power was heady though short-lived.

"Why you son-of-a-gun!" Speech finally released Toad from the spell. Here at last was something he could understand. "Trying to rob me, was you! And thinking you could have got away with it, huh? Wal, it's about time you learned something fer yore own good. Ain't nobody, *nobody*, in these hyar hills can cheat Toad Hood. And them that thinks they can, they got a lesson coming to 'em."

Punk measured the distance from where he stood to the timber back of him. Once he lit out and placed himself in those woods, he'd be as hard to find as Old Two-Toes when he denned up. His mind became as active as a water bug as he tried to figure out how long it'd take him to reach there. Would he have a long enough head start? Because he'd need it, as Toad's legs were longer

than his. But his backing up wasn't giving him any advantage because Toad was advancing all the time. So Punk halted. Resolutely, he faced up to his day of judgment.

Toad spit in his hands and then bent and wiped them in the dirt of the road, never once taking his eyes off his intended victim. As he rubbed his hands together, a gritty sound of dirt and sand was plainly audible. There was a crackle and a soughing of the leaves as Spider dropped from his perch and hunched himself down beside the road to watch.

Punk was completely off guard when he got a wham up against his head that rocked him back on his heels. At the same time, Judd let out a dreadful ear-splitting howl, the kind a dog would give over a fresh-dug grave.

Desperately, Punk flung himself at Toad's knees and, catching him unaware, laid him out flat in the dust of the road. And not for a second losing his gain, he straddled him and let his fists fly. The moment was sweet, but again, short.

Toad's bulk was too much for the smaller boy. He was rolled off onto his back and then delivered into the hands of the devil. Dark and desperate thoughts took hold of him as he received a merciless cuffing, kicking and battering. There was no getting away. Pinned to an unyielding earth, he was unable to free himself of the savage on top of him. How long it went on, he never knew.

"Aw, Toad, hon," a voice reached through to him as fists slackened, "I wouldn't keep on a-doing that if I was you. I shore wouldn't. A nice little feller like Billy Bunn hyar. T'aint fittin' to keep on a-mauling him. It shore ain't. And him a-bleeding like a stuck pig."

Punk's vision cleared enough so that he could make out the figure of Ma Hood. She stood over him, a stout angel of mercy, who had been a long time in getting there.

Wide-hipped, red-faced, and kindly, she bent down to him. "Git yorself up, Billy Bunn. I jes got the sweet rolls out of the oven. An' I baked a extry few in case we'uns had company. Dust yorself off, young 'un, and come on in."

It was a surprise to Punk that he was in one piece, but he hung together pretty well when he picked himself up. And he could walk, too, if floating were walking. It was a pure marvel that he could make it to the shanty. But he did. And he felt a wet, cold rag on his face and after a while he was aware he was eating sweet rolls and drinking hot coffee. And from the sounds of chewing close by, so were Toad and Spider. "You, ole boys, you," Ma Hood's voice was still gentle, "it just might happen that yore ma won't be of a mind to cook them pig-hocks fer yore supper."

"Aw, Ma," Toad's voice was downright plaintive. And the sudden movement from Spider, a rustling of his clothing, added a protest, too.

"Well," she considered for a spell, "I jes might go on and cook 'em if I was plumb shore this li'l ole boy went along home all in one piece."

"Shucks, Ma, we ain't aiming to do nothing to him," avowed Toad.

Punk couldn't help but wonder what else there was to do to him, unless they took his old bones and laid them out in the woods to rest. He was sure plumb tuckered, and how he'd ever make it home through the woods, he didn't know.

But he knew he didn't have the Hood boys to worry
about now. Easygoing Ma Hood had seen to that. All he
had to worry about was wondering if his legs had the
strength to carry him all the way home. But he faced up
to it. And he thanked Ma Hood politely for the sweet
rolls and coffee. And then, not knowing exactly how, he
was outside the shanty and under way. It wasn't but a
little while later that he was in the deep coolness of the
big trees.

Maybe he was out of his head, maybe he was. But it
was just as if the big trees were singing him a lullaby, the
kind his mother must have sung to him when he was a
scrap of a baby, not knowing that the mark of death was
already on her and that she'd be taken from her baby afore
he was walking.

He knew all about mother love from the wild creatures
in the timber land. He'd seen the old sow coons with their
kittens, parading them proudly in the moonlight: taking
them down to the water's edge for coon vittles. And there
was the wolf, risking her life in the farmyards, catching a
hen and toting it off to the den for her cubs. And the fox,
she'd go hungry herself just to provide for her family.
Come rain, sleet, or storm; come man, gun, and dogs, the
young were cherished and protected. And why his mother
had been taken from him, he'd never understand. All he
knew was the lonesomeness and the hungering and the
questions that raked him and always the eternal beating
of his boy heart, "I've got no one . . . no one. . . ."

Still, there was Granny, and she'd be thinking he was
dawdling in the woods if he didn't get on home. His head
dizzy, and his legs trembling, it was growing more dif-

ficult to push himself on. And he almost quit except for
the small nagging voice inside his head that said sharply,
"You, Punk, get the slack out of your pants, and hustle
on here." So, with another great effort he made it to the
edge of Horseshoe Lake where he fell down, giving himself
up to the blackness that reached out and gathered him in.

When he came to himself, the timber had bedded itself
down in nightfall shadow. He lay in the snug warm spot,
the spot warmed by himself, and listened. He liked the way
the timber came to life at night. With the first shades of
dusk, there was a stir, a rustling, and a breathing; and then
like a whisper that grows, the timber is awake. Now, the
big hoot owls, the sentinels of the dark, began calling back
and forth.

"Whooo . . . who's . . . in . . . the timmm . . . ber . . .
whooooo?" they asked.

And answers came from all sides, above the boy, from
the right of him, and to the left. Like Indian drums they
were, like echoes in a deep well, like mumbled witch talk.

The frog chorus down at the lake's edge made up a song.
And suddenly, a wildcat screamed and rent the air with
his rage. A fox, way off on the farthest hilltop, bayed
and bayed. It was a song of hunger. And just above the
boy, out on a limb overhead the whippoorwill set up his
refrain of *whip-poor-will, whip-poor-will.* . . . Well, that
was his name, Poor-will, and he'd been whipped a-plenty.
*Poor-will . . . poor-will.* . . .

As still as frozen creek water he lay. His heart beat
and thudded against the earth. A soothing solace seeped
into his bruised body.

More sounds came to him. Way off there were storm

warnings, a rumbling overhead like potatoes rolling in the attic. Was Hummy's Old Man upstairs rolling them about? Light split the sky and flashed. Had the Door opened a crack to let out the light? And he heard the patter of raindrops; at first a spit, a sputter such as fire gives off when water strikes it; a lull, then the drops fell heavier.

A wind blew up, rustling and crying like a child. It was trying to trick him. It seemed to call to him, "Billy Bunnnn . . . Bil-leee . . . Bunnn. . . ." afar off.

And now, his eyes were playing him tricks. There was a light moving and bobbing along the edge of the lake. Kind of looked like a lighted lantern and yet it could be a will-of-the-wisp light, said to spook men out of their wits. He kept his eyes on it, as it grew brighter and lighter, and nearer and nearer. The voice was a human voice. He managed to pull himself up into a sitting position and call out, "Here, I'm here."

The arms that reached out for him fair squeezed the living daylights out of him.

"Oh, Punk, I've found you!" It was his granny's voice. "I never should have sent you off with that collar!" And Punk found his head to be cushioned against a tender warmth of breast. He knew himself to be dreaming. Even so, he let his body sag heavy against the refuge. He felt himself hugged and rocked and sung to, a kind of lullaby, a sweet-sounding mother lullaby. And he fell asleep.

Yet later he remembered walking and staggering and the gentle hand that urged him on: and, last, the feel of cool sheets and the mattress under him.

Daylight reached in and shot cruel rays into his eyes,

forcing them to open and blink against the light. For the first second, he looked about in puzzlement, not recognizing the place he was in. He wasn't in his loft, nor in his own bed. He frowned and tried to figure out just where he was. Comprehension was a long time in coming, but finally, at last, it came to him. He was in the cabin. He was in Granny's bed. Granny's bed? Never in all his life could he recollect sleeping in her bed. He stirred and moaned in surprise at the thousand pricks of pain.

"You, Punk!" It was Granny all right, her voice sharp as usual. "How you feeling?"

Punk felt his bones and touched his face gingerly and at the same time wondered. He wondered about a great many things. But they were so jumbled up he couldn't sort them out. He figured he'd do it later when his head was clearer.

"I guess I feel all right," he at last managed.

"Humph." Granny's reply made it plain she wasn't believing him.

And then as carefree as the thistledown that drifted on the fall breeze, he floated away from Granny and the cabin and he was out in the timber.

He was the hawk on wing, flying sky-high, looking for a likely place to settle down. Suddenly, he saw himself above a large sycamore tree that stood close to a cabin. He knew it to be Hummy's place. And silently, as quietly as dusk falls, he let himself sweep along, yielding at last to the desire to rest for the night.

"Wake up, boy!"

The voice was new. It jarred him from his smooth flight and he resented it. But he opened his eyes and looked, of all things, right into the probing stare of Old Doc.

"Punk, you been sick." It was a statement that kneaded him into awareness. All Punk wanted was to get back to being the hawk on wing. But how could he? The Doc was shaking him and being pretty rough for a feller that was so knowing about cuts and bruises.

"Punk, you listen to me! Don't you want to get well? Get well and do things?"

He lazily took hold of that and examined it. Couldn't think of a thing he wanted to do but drift.

"How would you like to go with Hummy into the timber on a coon hunt? Maybe track Old Two-Toes?"

Hummy? Coon hunt? Old Two-Toes? His drifting came to a stop. But he guessed he hadn't heard right. Granny had a grudge against coon hunting, against menfolks a-skitting off to the woods, a-traipsing off from chores and learning and duty. Guess he had a fever. Guess he was plumb out of his head.

"Punk!"

Cracky, but her voice jarred him. It was taut as a fiddle string, it was sharp as a thin-edged rock.

"Ma'm?"

"You hear me, Punk?"

"Yes'm."

"You drink this hot broth, every last drop, mind you, and take Old Doc's medicine and get a good resting sleep!"

He was of a mind to pull the covers up over his head and shut out that do-this, do-that voice of hers. Still, a woman's voice could be mighty consoling when a body was sick and alone in the woods. It sure could be. Like now, the voice that was close to his ear, talking low and sweet to him. It was saying something he'd a mind to listen to.

"Comes a time when a boy must run, Punk. And you're going to have your run."

He looked into the dark eyes of his stepgranny that were right on the same level as his now. They were bright and shiny and penetrating. They held him earthbound. And they weren't of a mind to let him close his eyes either. They wanted something from him. He listened carefully then.

"I aim to let you be . . . the fox in the brush . . ."—her voice quavered but her eyes held steady—"the hawk on wing. . . ." She broke off and waited for his understanding.

"The deer in the wild meadow," he finished it for her.

They looked long at one another. He saw her nod her head, satisfied. He had given her the answer she wanted.

# 3

# Down Big Honey Creek Way

The second bottom of Big Honey Creek, where Hummy's cabin stood, wasn't so far from Granny's if you measured it by the way the crow flies. But if you followed Turkey Trail, the distance was considerable. And Punk found this fact to be real pleasurable. 'Course he was beholden to his stepgranny for setting him free a spell. Now he and Hummy were just menfolks with no fault-finding woman to boss them.

Life was the way it should be for a boy who had passed his twelfth borning day: running through the timber, free and wild, swinging from the grapevines, sprawling in the dirt, swimming naked in the creek water! Nary a worry in the world did he have. Oh, there might be a slight worrisome nip that took hold of a fellow when things were quiet, say at bedtime. Not much, but still it was there, put there by something Hummy had said.

Out of a clear sky, he'd said, "Had me a granny woman once. Boylike, I never set much store by her. She was everlastingly after me. And I was eternally making things troublesome as a young 'un will. Now, I see things different, and I got one repining."

He'd fallen silent then like he was way back in the past. And when he had his last say, he was looking deep into the boy's heart.

"I sure wish I'd kissed her now and then. I sure do."

And maybe he, Punk, should have kissed his granny when he was leaving. In all likelihood, he might have, too, if she hadn't been running through the whole book of Scriptures.

Cracky, she'd sowed, reaped, and harvested, while Hummy and his hounds had waited by the door.

It sure had rankled him, her woman-fretting before Hummy. Treating him like he was a tied-to-a-apron-string boy instead of Punk Bunn, grandson of old Billy Bunn. Frittering away words that had no place in the world where he was going: the world of hunting, fishing, trapping, and man pleasures.

Well, it was plumb foolish of him to let his thoughts stray back to the hill and the vexing problems that beset him there. He was here now, free, in the one place he wanted to be.

"Wild columbine, trumpet vine, and honeysuckle bring the hummingbirds back every year," Hummy told the boy. "Bright colors, sweetness, and prettiness will sure bait just about anything: bees, birds," he had grinned as he added, "menfolks!"

Punk knew he meant that last part for him. It explained the hankering he had for pretty things; whether it was sunlight on the meadow, or a flower-trimmed hat for his granny.

"Jewel weeds will bring a hummingbird from miles. And nasturtiums—ain't no feast any more appetizing than nasturtiums."

And the blaze of color about the cabin would trap a hummingbird, would reach out to a boy and fair rock him off his feet. Wasn't any place on the Ridge like Hummy's place. The boy lay under the sprawling cottonwood and again marveled at the loveliness brought about by man and nature.

Hummy had never taken a jaunt any place that he hadn't found some plant to be carefully uprooted and brought back to his cabin site to be bedded down. There were all kinds of ferns, lacy and dainty; fronds lifting proud heads in their easy-growing shady places. Toadstools and queer bits of green stuff, together with moss and button mushrooms ringed themselves about the old cottonwoods. And there were row upon row of wild flowers along the path and back of the cabin. Some were long past blooming, such as bluebells, birdfoot violets, sweet williams, the fragile lady-slippers, Dutchman's-breeches, jack-in-the-pulpit. But there were other varieties.

And right in the center of all this sat the cabin, a man's castle. It leaned kind of crooked up against a large sycamore tree as if it gained support that way. But the tree leaned, too, so that one couldn't be sure which was supporting the other. One of the lower limbs stretched out over the rooftop and rested there in leafy ease. Didn't take much extra looking to see that each was part of the other, same as . . . well, a boy's heart to his body.

The cabin was bleached, cottonwood color, what one

could see of it. The vines had sure taken over. Grapevines
trailed across the long front porch, windows were framed
in trumpet vine and Virginia creeper, all growing wild and
unrestrained. Honeysuckle climbed the tree trunk and hung
from the lower limbs in twisted loops.

Punk closed his eyes against the brightness of the day,
letting himself drift pleasantly into a drowsiness. Life was
sure easy here. It made Granny's turn of mind seem foolish.
Dog take it, why did Granny have to be so worrisome?
Why. . . .

"Run and get your gun, Billy Bunn, Billy Bunn! Run
and get your gun, Billy Bunn. . . ." It was Hummy breaking into his daydreaming with a song.

Instantly, Punk was on his feet.

"Do you mean it, Hummy? Do you mean it? Do you?"

But Hummy wasn't finished with his song, "You and
me together, we'll have us some fun, down in the woods,
Billy Bunn!"

"Well, now, I wouldn't be saying one thing and meaning another, would I?"

"But, Hummy, you said, 'Get your gun!' "

"Seems like I did, for a fact."

Punk felt a shiver go up his spine. He was so excited
he began to jig up and down. Hummy had been promising
him for a long time that when he was old enough he'd
let him have his grandpappy's rifle. And the time was here!

"B'jiggered if you don't act like a tom turkey stepping
on hot coals!" laughed Hummy, and to the boy's delight,
he began a ridiculous wild gobbler strutting, lifting his
feet high, stretching his neck out, and gobbling wildly.

It threw the whole place into confusion. The hounds

came on a dead run from in back, heads up, each giving voice in his own fashion: Red, baying deep down, Melly, high-pitched, and Old Blue uttering short yelps.

Even after he stopped his clowning, the dogs couldn't settle down. They were all stirred up and anxious. They kept whinnying and padding about, cracking their tails the way Granny snapped her driving whip.

"Yes sirree," Hummy continued when he got his breath, "we're sure going to give these lazy hounds a real run tonight."

It seemed as if the hounds could understand what Hummy was saying. They began loping around in circles, sniffing the air, and rumbling down deep in their throat in dog talk.

Hummy winked at the boy.

"Can't beat a old Missouri hound dog for knowing it all. Reckon they know what I'm about to say, before I open my mouth."

Old Blue let out a bawl as if he were on a hot trail.

"Talk it up, boy, talk it up," urged Hummy to his dog. "Tell them old coons out in the timber they better watch out tonight. Yes sirree, they sure had."

"Why tonight, why tonight?" Punk didn't feel himself to be as knowing as the hounds, and besides, he wanted to hear Hummy tell it all.

"Well," Hummy answered, "it's going to be a varmint-running night for sure, that's why. That old moon don't aim to show herself till nigh one in the morning. And all the varmints know it and they're figuring on running and feasting. Won't be no shadows out to shy 'em."

Punk felt so good that he let out a wild whoop and threw himself on top of Red. Both dog and boy hit the ground in a tangle of legs. They rolled and wrestled one another, the dog letting out deep growls as if any minute he'd tear that crazy little old Billy Bunn into chunks. Of course, Melly and Old Blue had to get in on it, too. They came in fast as if they were getting in on the kill. And quick as a coon's shake, the dogs had him squalling for help. Hummy just stood and grinned while the hounds clambered all over the boy, worrying and pulling at him like he was a no-'count possum.

He didn't seem to be in any hurry to stop it. And Punk sure got a wooling before a long arm reached down into the fracas and lifted him up, setting him on his feet.

"Reckon we'll need some of that vinegar for the trail," he said after shushing up the dogs. "No use on tuckering yourself out if we aim to get as far as Dynamite Gulch tonight."

Dynamite Gulch! Punk drew in his breath. He felt suddenly as if things were happening too fast. As long as he could remember, he'd been promised that someday he could go to Dynamite Gulch. But he hadn't ever thought that the time would come.

He flicked a glance at Hummy. But Hummy was acting as if nothing in the world were different; that Dynamite Gulch was as ordinary as Willow Branch or Coon Rock or Turkey Trail. He was ambling along to the cabin, whistling in a careless fashion.

Punk followed him slowly while his thoughts raced and twirled about in his head in crazy rotation. The time had come. Hummy said so. Not only was he going to get to use his grandpap's gun, but he was going to the very place where Death had pounced and taken both his menfolk, leaving him an orphan boy. Rocky Gulch, the place had been called before the accident. But after the terrible trouble, the Ridge people had named it Dynamite Gulch and that's what it would remain till the end of time.

"You, Punk!" Hummy's voice pulled him back to the present time. "Get the slack out of your pants."

Boy and man looked at each other and grinned. And just for a second, the feeling was there, as if the pestering granny woman was in the cabin with them. Punk ran a hasty hand through his hair, trying to bring some order to it. Cracky, not even the miles that lay in between them and this stepgranny could rid him of her bossing ways. Like now, he'd have to give his hair a good wetting down and combing before they started out.

"Looks like I got me a do-dawdler for a pardner, it sure do," Hummy was saying as he busied himself about the cabin, getting the camping gear together. "Now, if I was a little ole red-headed boy what was figuring on going out into the timber for a night or two, I'd think about sleeping out on the ground and about a hungry stomach. I would, for a fact.

"I'd be sure I had me a cutting ax in my belt and a knife in my pocket. Then I'd make certain I had plenty of hulls for my gun. And seems if I was wanting a batch of catfish to eat some night for supper, I'd have me some hooks and some twine."

All the time he was talking, he was laying out each piece of gear and the boy was happily stowing it away on himself. It was mighty comforting to know that Hummy was so smart about things. A body wouldn't have nary a fear being in the deep timber with such a woodsman as Hummy.

"Mighty important it is for a fellow to know how to

take care of hisself," Hummy was saying. "Sometimes it can be the difference between life and death. It sure can. And the only ways a body is going to learn how to take care of hisself is doing it."

Now wasn't that sensible? And it was exactly what he'd been telling Granny. But try and reason with a woman. Funny how different the female in the animal world was. She was the one who took the young ones out and showed them all the dangers of the land. But a granny woman kept a boy cooped up in a place, wasting his time with so many foolish things such as everlasting washing up and book learning and Bible reading and manners, b'golly! Oh, it was plain she was bound and set on making "something" out of him. And like as not, the "something" would never amount to a hill of beans in the woods. It was sure lucky he had Hummy who could show him how to take care of himself.

He watched carefully as the man reached for an old sack and commenced shoving in a variety of things: a piece of salt pork, a frying pan, salt, sugar, ground coffee, corn meal, and an old battered pot. He saw that Hummy was keeping the load light, "so as not to take the spring out of a fellow's knees."

"Reckon we'll need something to wrap up in on the creek bank. Can't ever depend on the weather, summer or not." He rolled up two old quilts, separately, into small rolls. One he swung off his shoulders and one he gave to the boy.

And the last thing he did before leaving the cabin was to reach up to the wall rack and take down the rifle and hand it over to Punk. The boy stood there, rifle in hand,

and a feeling of growing taller came over him. Inch by inch, foot by foot, and he was crowding the sky!

Hummy took one last look about the place and then he moved Punk along and out the door. There wasn't any more fuss than that in leaving the cabin. He just pulled the door shut, not locking it, nor barricading it in any way.

They took the Willow Branch way, the hounds splashing along through the shallow water, preferring it to the path the man and boy were taking. It was a lazy day and Hummy was setting his stride accordingly. Punk couldn't help but be a little put out that their gait was so leisurely. Dog take it but they'd be days getting to Dynamite Gulch at such a rate. He tried walking beside the man but the path was too narrow for both of them. And when he fell back and followed, he kept charging ahead and bumping into Hummy.

"Had me a crazy young hound pup once," Hummy said after they'd gone a ways and the boy was still stepping on his heels, "that was always wanting to run. Had to be ahead of the older hounds. Used to have regular running fits, he did. He'd run until he'd fall down. Couldn't learn him a thing."

Punk felt bad. He sure hadn't expected his friend to pull one of Granny's tricks on him, such as preaching. But sure as apples grew on trees, Hummy's story was going to end up with a lesson of some sort. Oh, he could sense it, the way a body could smell rain in the east wind. Heck. Started off like it was going to be a whopping good dog story, too. Well, he wasn't going to bite. He wasn't going to ask what happened to that pup with the running fit, he sure wasn't. . . .

"I suppose that crazy old hound pup ran himself to death," Punk said crossly.

"Nope." And Hummy kept on walking, his stride the same, light and easy. He moved silently, like an Indian, like a panther, like a real woodsman. It was a downright joy to watch him even if they weren't getting any place fast.

The boy tried to make his gait as leisurely. He shortened his step. And then he was bouncing like a hoptoad. Dog take Hummy. Wasn't he going to finish that story?

"What happened to that ole pup?"

"Broke his neck," Hummy answered. "Was running one day to get ahead of the older hounds and ran hisself right over the edge of the Gulch and fell and snapped his neck . . . *Crrrrk!* Like that."

Punk had to laugh. He'd sure asked for it. Walked right into the trap, he had. Of course, that ole pup had to come to some bad end if a boy was to learn a lesson.

"Tell you what." Hummy dropped down underneath a sprawly cottonwood, leaned his back up against the trunk, pulled out his pipe, filled it and lighted it. He took a couple of puffs before going on. "All the preaching in the world won't learn a feller a thing. It's like I said, the only way to learn a thing is by doing it."

"Now you, Punk, are fretting yourself out because we aren't making faster tracks. You're thinking we'll never get any place."

Punk grinned sheepishly. Wasn't any use denying it.

"Well now," he pulled hard on his pipe, "you know where the old camping ground of the Indians is."

The boy nodded. It was halfway between Hummy's

place and Dynamite Gulch and as far as Punk had ever traveled in the timber.

"We'll split up, you and me. Right here and now. And we'll meet at the camping grounds. You travel at the speed you want, and I'll come along at the gait I've set, same as now. And we'll see who gets there first."

"Is it a trick?"

"Nope."

Punk put on his thinking cap. He examined the proposition from every angle. "Can I run?"

"Yep."

"Take short cuts?"

"Yep."

"Heck, that's too easy."

"Might be," acknowledged the man. "Then again, might not."

Punk felt pretty smug. Looked as if he was going to have a chance to teach somebody a lesson. It was a pleasure-giving speculation, too. Wasn't ever a time he could recall when a young 'un could teach a grownup something. And now here was a chance, so easy it was like picking a possum off a persimmon limb.

"Punk." Hummy was a mild-spoken man and his voice was summery and calm. The boy pricked up his ears. Everyone in and around the Ridge knew that he'd better keep his ears peeled when Hummy Humphreys started talking easy like. "Before I turn you loose, I got to remind you of one thing. You and me have a obligation, and it's weighing on my mind. We got to get you back to your granny all in one piece. Reckon she's had enough heartache in this world without us adding to it."

Punk was all fired up to get started and he did hope Hummy wasn't going to sidetrack him, or change his mind about letting him prove who could beat the other. Of course, he'd often wondered about the bitterness in his stepgranny's soul but right now he was more interested in getting under way.

"Lordy goodness!" laughed the man, "that running fit is sure taking a-holt of you. Might as well let you go I guess. But there's one thing I got to tell you, son. Many a thing can happen between here and the camping grounds. Things to hold you up and make you lose time."

"Hummy," Punk was very positive, "there won't be nothing to keep me from getting there ahead of you."

"Larky as a little old bantam cock, now, ain't you? Well, I've still got to tell you. You have to figger on accidents and running into trouble, man-made trouble, and on the unexpected."

"When do we start?"

Hummy threw up his hands in mock despair, seeing how his words had gone in one ear and out the other. "Get going, son, get going," and he leaned back against the tree trunk as if he was fair frazzled out.

Punk toed the mark, ready to sprint ahead. "Come on, Hummy! We got to start at the same time if it's going to be fair play."

Hummy opened his mouth to say something and then he closed it. Without another word, he rose to his feet. He eyed Punk and then nodded his head at him.

With a wild whoop, Punk was off, running through the underbrush like a deer. It was such a fast start that he didn't have time to get his proper bearings and the first thing he knew he ran into a blackberry thicket. Cracky, but it was a chuckle-headed thing to do. It took quite a bit of doing to get untangled and to back out. He wasn't real certain whether Hummy would have called this an accident or the unexpected. But there was one thing he was sure of, he'd acted as crazy as that ole hound pup with the running fit.

He settled down into a fast trot, holding his elbows close to his side. He was in the big oak tree part of the timber; massive-trunked, heavy-limbed, old trees. Their glossy leaves made deep, black shadows. In some places, not even a sliver of sunlight could get through. And there was a stillness in the place that was kind of scary; lonesome, too. It was right easeful to know a body was on friendly terms with the Old Man upstairs.

He came across a narrow, hard-packed trail. It had been made by the deer and the wild life there in the woods. He knew where it led; right to the crossing of the Branch. He could make good time here. And he spurted ahead. Run, run, run!

His feet made quick, sharp sounds. It startled a bob-white up from the ground and the whir of wings made a ghostly noise. A rabbit shot across his path. There was a flash of red in a tree overhead as a squirrel raced for safety. A crash over in the heavier foliage indicated the presence of another animal.

The boy felt as if he had wings, he was covering the ground so fast. He couldn't helping thinking about Hummy with that poky old stride of his, going down the Willow Branch path. Punk figured he was way ahead of Hummy by now. And it was a good thing he was. He was getting winded. Well, he'd made so much time, he'd set awhile and get his breath back.

Right off the path was heavier shade, dark as night shadows. He made his way to it, walking carefully, watching for rotten logs or holes. With the race so nearly won, wasn't any use in taking chances on accidents such as a twisted ankle. He'd lost a bit of time there in the blackberry patch but he'd made it up. And the way he looked at it now, there shouldn't be anything to worry about between here and the camping grounds. Hummy was sure as cautious as an old granny in the woods. "You got to figure on trouble, man-made," he'd said. Now, just what kind of man-made trouble could a boy run into? The Indians had long been gone. And there weren't any more of the bushwacking parties or the raiders that used to sweep down on their hills. And. . . .

Way off, came the sound of a hound. Punk listened. A good woodsman could always name a hound by his voice. It wasn't bugle-voiced like Melly, nor deep-mouthed like Red or Old Blue. It plainly wasn't. Wasn't anything pleasing about his voice. There was only one dog who made such a coarse, rough kind of bawling, and that was Judd, Toad Hood's hound!

Punk took to cover. A scared rabbit couldn't have made faster tracks. He dropped onto his hands and knees and scurried under the limbs of the water oak beside him. The limbs were so heavy with foliage that they touched the ground.

Underneath was like being in an immense Indian tepee with the tree trunk same as a tent pole. He could stand up straight farther in. It was cool and dark. And it would sure offer him protection from human eye. But would it be cover enough from a hound dog's nose? Punk doubted it. Cracky, to meet Judd with Toad and Spider way off here in the timber would be pure disaster. Wasn't time to make a getaway. Besides, they were coming from the direction he had to go if he were to meet Hummy at the camping grounds.

Wasn't much time to try and outwit them, either. The sounds were coming closer. Punk made a quick dash out from under the tree over to a nearby one. He scrambled up the trunk and then worked his way back down, keeping himself in the same course. He was putting the tree-tapping trick into actual use. There was a chance that his tactics might fool Judd.

Then he hurried back under the big water oak. Leaping from the ground, he caught hold of a limb and swung up onto it, settling down to wait. My, but his heart was pounding. It was a regular thunder in his ears. Now wouldn't it be a joke on him if he couldn't hear them and they passed right by without stopping and here he'd be sitting up in the tree as silly-looking as a hoot howl and. . . .

"Consarn you, Judd!" Toad Hood's voice wasn't more than an arm's throw from the water oak where Punk was hiding. "Shut up that racket!"

They were here! Needn't have worried about not hearing them; nor their passing on by. No such luck for him. Hadn't he pointed out to himself time and time again, he was the unluckiest guy on the Ridge?

Through his screen of leaves he could see Toad and Spider, who had halted on the path while their hound dog was kind of milling around at the spot which he, Punk, had left a few seconds ago. Judd's hair on the back of his neck was all ridged. He was making ugly rumbling noises in his throat as he sniffed the ground, working over every inch of the place where Punk had been.

"Whatcha smellin' out, now? Old Two-Toes?" Toad's snort of derision wasn't too pleasant. "Ain't nothin' but these hyar traps going to catch that old booger. Ain't that right, Spider, huh?"

In reply, Spider rattled the steel trap he was carrying. Punk could hardly contain himself, he was so mad. A steel trap! No one set traps in the summertime. The animals all kind of knew this and weren't nearly as wary as they were in the winter. It was a dirty, lowdown, ornery thing to do.

"Yep, the Hood boys always even up the score, now don't they, Spider?"

Spider's bare feet slapped the ground in quick response as he bobbed his head up and down.

"An' no coon's gonna outsmart the Hood boys, are they, Spider?"

Spider's head went from left to right in violent shakes.

"Reckon we'll larn old Mr. Two-Toes! It'll be old Mr. Has Been when we git this last trap set at Coon Rock. We'll fix that smarty coon for sure this time."

Judd let out a bawl. It was a trailer's cry. It meant he'd at last picked up a scent. And Punk knew right away whose it was.

"Whatcha found, mutt?" Toad's voice was mildly interested.

Punk froze to the limb. This was it. Unless his trick worked, he was sure in for it. And suddenly, that tree-tapping trick seemed mighty flimsy.

"Sick 'em! Sick 'em!" shouted Toad as Judd again let out a roar.

The hound whirled and circled on the spot, snuffing and grunting as he worked his way over to the water oak. He was beside himself with excitement. The Hood boys began to think there was big game about and they were close at the dog's heels. For a second, agonizing to Punk, Judd circled under the limb Punk was on. Then hitting the trail that led to the other tree, Judd took off. He ran straight to the tree trunk and jumped up on it, baying and taking on.

"He's got something treed! He's got something treed!" shouted Toad. "Climb up there, Spider, and jump it out."

Punk could hear Spider scrambling up the tree. Judd was still howling. Suddenly there was the sound of a limb being shaken and a falling noise that ended in a loud thump on the ground.

Punk couldn't see any of it. He just heard Toad cussing and kicking the dog away from whatever it was.

"Damned old possum!" Toad bellowed. "Come on down, Spider."

Judd gave a howl as Toad fetched him a kick in the ribs.

"That'll larn you! Keep off them possum tracks. We're after coon, you old fool!

"You, Spider, hurry up there. We'll make tracks for Coon Rock. Shake a leg!"

Punk couldn't believe it. Was he going to get off this easy? Would the Hoods and Judd leave this part of the timber and go on about their business, leaving him all in one piece? Cracky, what had brought about this miracle?

Had it been entirely his tree-tapping trick or had the Old Man upstairs had a hand in it?

Punk dropped down from the tree still feeling pretty shaky. He didn't waste any time in getting away. He shot out onto the path, thanking his lucky stars that the Hoods were off in the other direction. Now it was really run, run, run! He'd have to make up for lost time. Golly, but it would be good getting back with Hummy. He'd have lots to tell him, too. And he guessed he was pure cured of his running fit. Not that he was ready to give up on winning. No sirree. He still aimed to get to the camping grounds ahead of Hummy. Even if he ran himself to death, he was plumb set on beating Hummy.

Down the path, he winged his way. Just let him win this time, and he'd be content to go at that slow and easy gait of Hummy's from now on till kingdom come. He sure would. Oh, he'd relish it in fact, the same way he was thinking about a drink of running creek water from Willow Branch.

A feeling of triumph began to rise in him. He'd cut the breeze, for a fact. It was only a little way yonder. A chuckle rose up in him as he thought of Hummy's surprise. The way he figured it, he, Punk would have just enough time to catch his breath and set himself down under a shady tree before Hummy would come ambling in with his hound dogs.

He rounded the path that ended up at the Indians' old camping grounds.

There, leaning up against the tree, cool as cistern water, was Hummy.

"What kept you?" he said, grinning.

## 4

# To Dynamite Gulch

Sunset was but a few seconds away when Punk and Hummy reached Dynamite Gulch. So that when the boy had his first glimpse of the Gulch, it was in a blaze of light. Limestone cliffs, cabin-sized boulders, cottonwoods, hickory and walnut trees, silver poplars, thickets of persimmon and buckeye saplings, were all swept by the glory of the sun.

From the high crest, where they had paused, one could see the entire depth and breadth of the ravine. Man and boy stood silently while Punk gazed and gazed. The sun seemed to grow larger, the color redder. The light shone with greater intensity.

It reached out and sparked the limestone rock, it fuzzed the treetops, kindled the shadows, ringed the boulders, fired the buffalo grass. The creek was a river of flame.

Then with the swiftness of a falling star, the sun set back of the facing ridge.

The hounds, who had been as silent as their menfolk, now lifted their heads and mourned: mourned for the departing light, mourned for the departed generations. It was a sad sound, their lament. It spoke of many things: of death and of life, of sorrow and heart anguish, of Time, and of forever and ever. Things that twisted and tore at a boy's heart and were past understanding. Left orphaned with no kin of his own; and who was to explain that?

"Shush it up, you hounds!" said Hummy. "That howling'll joggle the rocks loose for certain."

Red and Old Blue quieted down. But Melly pitched her voice higher. Her lament drifted out over the ravine, starting up the echoes like sleigh bells on a frosty night.

"Now ain't that pretty. I just bet the angel Gabriel himself got no prettier notes than that in his horn." And Hummy reached out and gave Melly a good whack on her head. "Now confound it, I told you to shush up. I declare, if it ain't just like a woman, always having to have the last say."

"Are you ready, Punk?"

Ready? The boy stood for a second looking off across the Gulch. This was the very moment he had been rushing to meet, all the days of his growing. Why as long as he could remember, he'd hankered for this time to come. And now a strange reluctance had hold of him. It was sure bewildering.

He turned and met Hummy's eyes. It was a direct, understanding look, a man to man look. All his doubts disappeared. His heart lost its heaviness and became light and gay.

He was right at Hummy's heels as they made the down-

ward descent into the Gulch. Down, down. It was like
plunging into a deep well. The coolness came up and
fanned their faces. The evening shadows made dark pools
for them to step in.

It took quite a bit of doing, getting to the bottom. But
after that, it was easier going. The ground leveled off
into a green valley. The evening light now gave a vaporous,
greenish cast to everything. Dusk was settling in. There
was barely light enough to make out the spot where
Hummy was heading. Punk saw it was close to the limestone cliff, a smooth cleared sort of a place, guarded by a
lone poplar. And right close by was the running creek
water.

"Looks like someone's been here afore us," Hummy said
pointing to the tracks on the sandy bank.

There as plain as anything was the footprint of Old
Two-Toes. Wasn't any mistaking that print: a coon track
with only two toes.

Hummy chuckled. "It'll take a mighty smart feller, a
lot smarter than Toad Hood, to get ahead of that ole
grandpappy coon."

The boy tingled as he leaned over studying the tracks.
Old Two-Toes, king of the coon clan, and Punk Bunn
were sharing the same creek bank together. It was a dream
that had come true.

They made camp there. And in a little while, they had a
fire going. As the first flame came into being, darkness fell
about them. It was as if the light had held just long enough
to let them get settled. Punk was glad for the crackle of
the flames. It was pure lonesome in the gully.

A soft wind was slewing through the poplar leaves

making a sighing sound like a woman's grieving, like Granny's despair for her menfolk.

Punk squatted down by the fire. He let the heat scorch his face, hoping it would take the chill off him. He was not aware of Hummy's sidewise glance. He was aware only of the funny feeling in the pit of his stomach.

"B'jiggered, but I'm plain gutted," said Hummy. "Got a queasy feeling in my stomach. Kind of like butterflies that's all gathered on a honey stump and their wings are flipping up and down, and their feelers are a-quivering. Brrrrrrrr!" and Hummy twitched and jerked himself from head to toe, mincing about in the firelight as dainty as you please. It was a comical sight.

Right away Punk began to feel better. He started laughing, half at the man and half at himself. Might have known he was hungry. Cracky, come to think about it, he hadn't had much at noontime, just some cold grub that Hummy had stashed away in the sack. Wasn't nothing wrong with him but what a little food would fix. And that ole wind could just keep on slewing through the leaves, making those sorrowful sounds. Reckon with grub in his stomach, he'd not pay a whit of attention to it.

"Yes, sirree," Hummy was saying, "for a fact now, my stomach is plain hollering for grub." He was pulling part of the burning wood out of the big fire, shoving it into a smaller one he was making at the side.

"Reckon I got a good surprise for someone in the way of food. Back yonder, while I was a-waiting on my do-dawdler pardner to show up. . . ." He cleared his throat, not looking once in the boy's direction. Punk had to giggle. It was the first time there had been any reference made to his beating Punk to the camping grounds.

"As I was saying," Hummy went on, "back yonder, while I was waiting on my pardner to show up, I seen a couple of ole red-tails a-stretched out on the tree limbs taking a snooze. And I says to myself, says I, fried squirrel for supper!" And he drew two nicely dressed young squirrels out of his sack and held them up for Punk to see.

"Nothing in this world's as savory as fried squirrel out in the woods." He paused and considered. "Unless it's fried catfish with corn-meal flapjacks." He became more thoughtful. "Or rabbit all stewed up in onions and tomatoes, or a young turkey turning on a spit with its juices dripping and sizzling into the coals."

"Stop, stop!" begged Punk, knowing himself to be as weak with hunger as a newborn calf.

All the time Hummy was talking, he was getting out his frying pan, making the fire the way he wanted it, and finally cutting the meat up into pieces. It was a pleasure to Punk to see how swiftly he worked.

In a short time, he had the squirrels on frying. And soon the air was filled with an aroma that made the glands in Punk's mouth run like crazy. The hounds began sniffing the air and padding about. Punk didn't see how he could wait. He just bet he could eat a piece raw, as hungry as he was.

"Rustle around, Punk, and get us some creek water," sang out Hummy. "Got to have us some coffee."

He kept the boy on a half run from then on with "Do this, do that." He could snap out orders as brisk as a certain stepgranny could. Oh, you could tell Hummy had been well-learned by a granny woman.

Did they eat supper unwashed and uncombed? They sure didn't. They washed their hands in the creek and laved their faces good and then ran a wet comb through their hair. Somehow out in the woods, Punk thought there plain wouldn't be any need of all this cleaning up. But the longer he was around Hummy, seemed like the more surprises there were in store for him. He was mighty finicky about cleanliness, that man was. Not that it lessened him in the boy's eyes. It simply drove home the fact to Punk that once a granny woman took hold of a fellow, she sure left her mark on him.

Cracky, but that cleaning up made Hummy look good. It gave him a polished look, like a clean blade on a hunting knife. The firelight touched the slicked-down graying hair, twinkling the water drops that hadn't fallen off, gleamed against the lean, tanned face. Punk felt that maybe Adam had been a disappointment to the Lord, but he just bet Hummy wasn't.

Wasn't anything that man couldn't do. Take this cooking out, now. Punk hadn't ever tasted meat as good as he was having. And the thin corn meal flapjacks with the sweetening pure melted in a boy's mouth. Oh, but it was good. And it was a marvel, the tricks that Hummy knew. To keep coffee from boiling over, he stuck a green stick in the pot; a pinch of soda would make the toughest meat tender; rust on a skillet was burned off in a hot fire; a pan never stuck if a body knew enough not to use water on it. Knowledge like Hummy's could never be found in a book. No sir, it sure couldn't.

And he had a speedy way of cleaning up when supper was over. The leavings went to the hounds. The skillet

was cleaned out with a handful of grass and then tossed on
the edge of the fire to burn clean. The coffee pot was
pulled to the side of the fire because they'd drink up the
rest of it later. It was all so simple living out-of-doors.

Punk threw himself on the ground and stretched out in
contentment. Guess he wouldn't change places with anyone in the whole world tonight. It was good to be alive.
And he reckoned he ought to be ashamed of the way he
was forever harping on his hard luck and all his past
troubles. Somehow, lying on the ground with the firelight
throwing a circle around the two of them and the sky
a-jumping with stars overhead, it made a fellow feel he
had blessings he hadn't been counting.

*Count 'em . . . count 'em,* sang out an old bullfrog on
the sand bar, just as if he knew what Punk was thinking
about. *Dig-deep, dig-deep,* he went on. And then a whole
frog chorus went, *I believe I kin . . . I believe I kin. . . .*

And sure enough he could. It was astounding how many
blessings he found he had when he set himself to count
them. Come to think about it, the very eyes that allowed
him to look up into the star-studded sky right now were
a wonder and a miracle—eyes that caught the sudden
flash of light that now streaked across the sky.

"Lightning?"

"A shooting star."

Cracky, a shooting star! The joy of living and breathing
took hold of the boy and fair strangled him. This was
Hummy's Old Man upstairs, for a fact, whose generous
hand could toss a star across the heavens to pleasure the
people below.

"Punk—" Hummy took his pipe from his mouth and

held it cupped in his hands while he talked. "There's lots of questions coming to a full boil in you."

Punk nodded. "For a fact."

"I figure it's time you had some answers." But the man shook his head at Punk's eager waiting. "T'won't be like doing your sums at school. You got to go way back at the beginning to figure out why a thing is. Maybe you don't find the answer, but you unravel some of the puzzling."

Punk eased his position on the ground and waited.

"Now, take your stepgranny, Eliza Jane," Hummy began. "There was a time when your granny was as pretty as a black-eyed daisy a-growing in the field and twice as sassy."

"Pretty?" Punk had a quick picture of her in her plain black bonnet and her black skirt, the way she looked on meeting day, and he had to shake his head.

"As true as I'm sitting here," Hummy told him. "And her hair was black and wavy, curling about her face, never staying put, making a regular gypsy out of her." His voice was low but it was reaching Punk's ears all right.

"She wasn't no bigger than my thumb. But she could outrun anybody at the school house and she could outride the best. And at square dancing, well, there weren't none on this Ridge could hold a candle to her. Many's the time I've swung her to the tune of the Bristle Ridge Twist."

Hummy dropped his hand down onto the ground beside him and gave the earth a couple of quick, hard pats. It became a rhythmic beat that stirred the pulse in Punk's throat. And then Hummy was calling the dance just as if the fiddles were a-strumming and the couples were sashaying up and down before them.

*"Join your holts and circle to the left,*
*Break your holts and circle to the right,*
*Your lady in the lead and the gents behind,*
*All eight balance and all eight swing.*
*On to your left, lady back to your right,*
*And on and around, left to the right,*
*Meet your pardner, swing and once around,*
*Now then, all the way around!*
*The first couple out and balance swing,*
*Then on to your right and circle four,*
*And half around and right on through,*
*Center couple swing, across the hall,*
*Now double the dose and hug her close!*
*Cross the hall, and circle four,*
*And ladies doe and gents you know,*
*Walk right through on your heel and toe,*
*Swing them by the elbow and back by the wrist,*
*And don't forget that Bristle Ridge twist!"*

Punk could hear the hands clapping to the called-out tune; he could hear the fiddle playing, and right off, he could see the whirling black-eyed Eliza Jane in a red ruffled petticoat!

It was pure magic the way Hummy made the past so real. He was calling up the ghosts from time back, and he had them whirling, and cutting pigeon wings; sashaying, circling, and promenading right before the boy's very eyes.

There was his grandpap, Billy Bunn, lean and dark, stepping high, wide, and handsome. ". . . reckless, devil-may-care men, the Bunns. Always had their pick of the women-folk. . . . And Eliza Jane, from the beginning, had her heart plumb set on Billy Bunn. . . ."

Hummy's voice kept on, unwinding the past, giving to Punk all the details of bygone days, of men and women long gone, of heartache and anguish. The scope of the story was wide. It was taking three generations, from old Billy Bunn up to his grandson, Punk. And he, Punk Bunn, was at last hearing the whole story of his own kinfolks. Why it was like a page from the Scriptures, the part from Genesis, "This is the book of the generations of Adam . . . and he begat a son in his own likeness, after his image. . . ."

And Hummy went way back into time, telling the boy how his grandpappy married Berrilla Bates: "No more like Eliza than a quail to a redbird." And how it sorrowed Eliza, embittering her, so that she turned to the Scriptures and the black bonnet and skirt.

Hummy's voice was like a harp and Punk felt the words he was hearing as sorrowful as the ballads sung by the Ridge people.

"But she finally married my grandpap, my stepgranny did."

Hummy nodded his head slowly. "To raise your pap, left motherless; to raise a young 'un who was whelped by another, so as to speak. And your grandpap out with the Claytons and the Gibsons, a-hunting with the dogs, restless and roving."

It was a lot to think about. Punk stared into the fire as if there he might find an answer to the puzzle life was. Why did it have to be all so mixed up? With all the pleasuring things about, why were there heartache and pain?

"And your papa, young Bill, when it came time for him to marry, he picked himself a pretty little thing named Doll Larimer. Had a face like a sweet pansy flower. Pretty as all get-out."

"Then young Bill Bunn begat a son in his likeness, after his own image," breathed Punk. "And that was me."

Hummy spoke softly. "So it was."

A piece of wood snapped in the fire and fell apart in a shower of golden sparks. And Hummy, being reminded his pipe was out, reached over for a bit of stick with glowing embers. It was a welcome pause for Punk. He already knew the part about his mammy being taken with the sickness and how his stepgranny had taken him to raise, the same way she'd raised his pap.

Stillness settled in. The frog chorus let up. The wind died down. The leaves of the silver poplar were silenced. But the thoughts that whirled about in the boy's head weren't silenced. They were going around and around like the figures in Hummy's square dance, sashaying and circling and doing a regular Bristle Ridge twist.

It was plumb perplexing how his stepgranny's face kept appearing before his eyes, she not being his kin by blood. Reckon a boy should have his mind on his own grandmammy, Berrilla, who had been taken before her time. And there was his own pap to think about—and his little mother, Doll. Tenderness swept over him as he thought about her and the sweet, pansy face. He was surely obliged to Hummy for giving him that picture.

Then back his thoughts swung to the vexing, pestering woman whose life had been frustration and despair. He thought about her alone in the cabin. He could see her, ramrod straight in the rocker, Bible in her lap, reading by the lamp. She'd probably be missing the rebellious boy who usually sat by the fireplace. It kind of bothered him.

It was a sobering thought that this stern, God-fearing

woman had once been sassy and gay: that the sparkling, bright Eliza Jane and his stepgranny were one and the same. Well, one thing he just bet, and that was if she ever put on a flower-trimmed hat and a calico dress, she'd be as pert as any granny woman on the Ridge. And it'd sure pleasure him to see her so.

The heavy breathing of the sleeping hounds reached him. Then he was aware of the murmur of the water in the creek behind him. It was as if he had been away from the Gulch and was now coming back to it. He became conscious of the hushed quality of the night as if it were waiting for the rest of the story.

He lifted his head and looked at Hummy. He was ready. He'd hear it all, every mournful word of it.

"On such a night as this," Hummy began, "old Billy Bunn and his son, young Bill, went hunting with the Claytons and my pap and me."

The words sparked out into the night. Like a golden shower of embers, they flashed into the boy's consciousness. At last he was to hear the story of the reckless, devil-may-care man, who roamed the woods at night to all hours, coming home only with the dawn. He'd hear of the hunting dogs and of the coons that ran the sand bars and the waterways, of their tree-tapping, and their matching wits with menfolks. And he'd hear of the companionship of men, and of their talk around a campfire, and of all the things a man-child hankered to hear.

"It was nigh ten years ago when the hunt took place. That'd make it the year . . . 1890; a long time ago to you, Punk, being a growing boy. But to me, seems like only yesterday." Again a sigh came from Hummy.

"My pap, he was in his eighties and could outwalk us
all: and the Clayton boys, Perrin and Stark, together with
the Bunns, the six of us made up the hunt.

"We had four crackerjack hounds; your grandpap's
black hound, Old Tom-Tom, leading the pack. He was
the trailingest dog in these parts. And his voice—well,
it had a trick of going way down deep and then giving
off a double sound, kind of an echo. Sounded like the
tom-tom drums of the Indians, and so he was named.

"Been trailing most the night. Had jumped us a big
old boar coon way back at Big Honey Creek and it'd been
nip and tuck all night, that plagued old coon outwitting
the dogs at every mile of the trail.

"Well, it got so we'd walked ourselves plumb out of boot
leather, all the way from back yonder to here. And the
hounds were pure crazy at being made such chumps. And
I might as well admit it kind of got under all our skins,
the way that coon kept fooling us.

"Your grandpappy was fit to be tied. And his hound,
Old Tom-Tom, well, he'd made up his mind he was going
to have that coon. Reckon the rest of us might have
called it quits, after so long a time, but Billy Bunn didn't
know that word.

"And he kept urging his dog on and we all saw it was
going to be a hunt to beat all hunts. It was going to be
a trail to the death . . . to the death. And so it was.

"Came all the way to Dynamite Gulch, or Rocky Point,
as it was called then, my pap still walking right along with
us. And it was then we finally got that coon treed: treed
him up in a big old oak tree, not far down the waterway
from here.

"Well, we built up a fire, just about where we're sitting now, getting back our breath and planning on how we were going to bag that coon. It was a powerful big tree and weren't none of us wanting to climb it and jump him out. Not after the long hike we'd had.

"And we felt good, the way men do when they've had a good hunt and they've got the upper hand. And we laughed and joked and sat around the fire, swapping stories and passing the bottle my pap had brought along. His snakebite medicine, he used to call it."

Punk hugged his knees tight against his chest. Oh, but he was sure beholden to Hummy for giving him this happy picture. It was the way he'd think of his grandpap and his pap from now on, sitting around a fire in the heart of the timber with their friends; hunting men, lean and bold, careless and free. In that picture, there was no heartache nor suffering. They were men who were talking and laughing. Nothing in the whole wide world as pleasure-some as hunting men to Punk's way of thinking. They were the men who took life and made it into an exciting adventure, knowing the joy and zest of living better than most. For what could match the thrill of stalking wild game; running the fox to his lair, tracking the deer, flush-ing the quail, trailing the wild turkey, stealing up on mallard ducks at the first streak of dawn? And that's what he'd remember about his menfolk, this freedom, this joy.

"I don't rightly recollect who thought up the sticks of dynamite. But I recollect t'was your grandpap had the sticks in his knapsack. Blowing up trees was no trick. We'd done it before.

"And this tree was old and its trunk was hollow. It'd

blow easy. So we tied up a bundle, an extra charge for good measure. And your pap, young Bill, being the youngest and quickest, was elected to throw it into the hollow and run back to safety.

"It was one of those freak accidents. Your pap lighted the fuse and pitched it into the tree trunk and turned to run. And in getting away, he caught his toe in a root and he fell to the ground, striking his head against a rock and stunning him. That's the way we figured it after.

"And afore any of us could move, your grandpap, fast as a panther, sprang to the side of his boy. And he had him up in his arms . . . had turned our way, when the charge went off. And the tree fell. And it caught them both."

Punk's ears were filled with a roaring. So must the timber have echoed to the discharge of the dynamite and the crash of the big tree. So must the walls of Jericho have sounded when they came tumbling to the ground. So must the sound have been to his stepgranny's ears when her world came crashing down about her. Tears wet his cheeks.

"I'm beholden to you, Hummy, for the story," he gulped.

And then he unrolled the quilt and lay down on it, close by the fire. Hummy, without a word, did likewise.

And the fire burned low, and the stars popped in the sky.

"Hummy?"

"Here."

"It was a brave thing my grandpap done."

"It was."

The boy lay very still and thought some more about

it. He didn't have to ask what caused a man to rush into the very jaws of death with no thought for himself. Guess he was old enough to know about love. And hadn't he heard enough about it in the Bible? But that word was a powerful mixed-up word. It could bring joy and it could bring sorrow. It could take a woman's heart and break it like an egg shell. It could take a man's life and cause him to give it up for another's. Such a longing rose up in his heart that for a second he was unable to speak. But at last he managed it.

"Would my pap have done the same for me?"

Hummy reached out and took hold of the boy's hand and held it firmly. "Yes. That's the way a man is made, Punk."

The wind came up the Gulch, stirring the poplar leaves again to murmuring and sighing. A whippoorwill called out across the dark. And as if in reply came the deep, booming cry of the owl. There was a movement close by as some varmint began to move about for night prowling.

All was astir, rustle and movement, except on the quilt. Punk was asleep.

## 5

# *Along Clearfork*

Sunup was sudden. Punk felt as if he had just closed his eyes for a second before opening them to the brightness of the morning. It was surely a pleasuring sight; the sun rising up out of the water downcreek. It seemed to be pulling the boy up out of his sleep as if by strings.

"You, Punk, you! Get the slack out of your pants," sang out Hummy, who was turning something in the skillet over the fire.

With a whoop, Punk rolled to his feet. Cracky, but he felt fine, wild and free-like. He couldn't hold it in. He wanted to run and holler. He wanted to reach up and snatch that old sun right out of the sky and run with it.

The cliffs just sassed him in reply and flung his whoop right back in his face. 'Course, Punk feeling his oats the way he did, was bound to have his say. And the Gulch rang with the boy's yells and the echoes, until suddenly

he felt himself seized and shucked right out of his under-
wear and ducked down in the cool creek water.

"By thunder," Hummy grumbled from the creek bank,
"won't be nary a bit of live meat left in this here Gulch.
Like as not everything's taken to cover. Had me a couple
of old bushy-tails spotted right over yonder piece as some
likely vittles." He paused to shake his head gloomily.
"Don't see hide nor hair of 'em now. Reckon they don't
aim to end up as stew, leastwise not today."

At the mention of vittles, Punk felt his stomach collapse
flat against his backbone. Golly, but he was plain gutted.
He sniffed the air. Something was smelling powerful
savory; a crispy, golden-brown smell.

"What smells so good, Hummy?"

"Channel cat."

"Channel cat?" Punk was puzzled. He hadn't seen any
signs of fishing.

"How come you got any fish?"

"Set me a limb line, that's what I did."

"A limb line!" Punk rolled to his feet and stood dripping
on the sand bar. He looked accusingly at the man. "Well,
where was I?"

Hummy laughed. "Lordy, lordy! Where was you? Why
sonny, there's just no telling where you was. Now to my
eyes you was asleep there on the quilt, but where you really
was only the Old Man upstairs knows."

Punk was plain put out that he'd missed the fun of
setting a limb line. He felt cheated, too. Chances were
he'd never get loose with Hummy again, Granny being
of the turn of mind she was.

It riled him that Hummy didn't see the importance of

passing along every single trick he knew of living off the woods and streams. Hadn't Punk told him often enough that living off the woods was exactly what he planned on doing someday?

"You could have woke me," he said reproachfully.

Hummy cast a flick of a glance at him. "Young 'uns need their sleep," he said mildly.

"Reckon I can get plenty of that when I go home." Punk couldn't explain it. He had turned quarrelsome. One minute he had been happy as a bluejay and now he felt as cross as a cornered coon. He stood stark naked, not making a move toward getting his clothes on.

"Lordy me," shouted Hummy looking up into the sky, "there's mister chicken hawk circling right overhead. Reckon he's trying to make up his mind what that white meat is a-standing on the sand bar. If'n I was a skinny ole boy, I'd make tracks for my duds. That's what I'd do."

But Punk was so swollen with worrisome thoughts that he couldn't move.

It was as if there were two of him. One was all dressed, standing over by Hummy with nary a care in the world; the other one was naked as the day he was born and mule-stubborn, rooted in one spot.

"Growing days," said Hummy out loud and to no one in particular. "Yes sirree, growing days. Mite skittish times."

He went over to the fire and eased himself down, careful-like, pulling the skillet of frying fish off to the edge of the flame. He was plainly making preparations to eat.

Punk was real sorry for himself. He'd gotten himself into a predicament he wasn't likely to get out of, 'less he had help. Turned to a pillar of salt he was, and like as not he'd be standing in that spot till kingdom come—for all Hummy cared, he would.

Just then, mister chicken hawk let out a screaming cry and dived low right over his head and the pillar of salt turned into a lively twelve-year-old boy scampering for his clothes.

Breakfast had an extra fine flavor. Seemed as though there had never been channel cat fried to such a crunchy turn. And while they were eating, Hummy told him how a limb line was set. Wasn't nothing hard about it. A line was tied to an overhanging limb of any tree that was close to the water's edge, a willow or an elm, maybe. Then the hook was baited with crawdad, or frog, or liver from wild game. Made it easier if a feller had a boat and came into the tree. But getting wet wasn't nothing to mind when he could dry hisself out at the wood fire.

The boy listened as Hummy talked, easy and slow-like, all the time wanting to say he was sorry for his behavior earlier. It shamed him to think how contrary he was. Lately, he sure didn't know himself: all churned up with a lot of mixed feelings. Hadn't been any sense in getting so uppity about the limb line. He tried to explain it to Hummy.

But the man just grinned. "Shuckings," he said, "t'weren't nothing at all. Most young things think they got to know everything at once. And don't matter whether they be a boy or a pup, they're all alike." He drained down his last drop of coffee and then dug down in his pocket for his pipe and tobacco. "Had me a greedy pup once," he began in a recollecting sort of way.

But Punk halted him. "No, no," he begged, half laughing and half tearful. "I'll be gol-derned if I want another lesson."

Both man and boy looked at one another, speechless.

"What's yore granny a-going to say about that?" Hummy finally got out.

Punk was bug-eyed. "Never aimed to say it. It just popped out."

Hummy laughed. "Well, let yore granny hear you say it and there'll be a ruckus made. Not that she ain't heard plenty of it in her day. Reckon there was no one could cuss better'n old Billy Bunn. When she taken you to raise, she 'lowed there'd never be another cuss word said." He pulled down on his pipe. " 'Course, out here with me, can't say as there's anything wicked about a little ole word like 'derned,' but women folks is mighty misunderstanding."

"Amen!" said Punk recklessly, not caring whether that was blaspheming or not.

Hummy shook his head. "Don't be getting too cocky," he warned. "Yore granny can whittle a man down to no bigger than a piece of shaving."

But who knew that better than Punk?

Right now he was wanting to know, "What happened to that greedy old pup of yours?"

"There now," Hummy shook his head, "if that ain't like a young 'un. First he don't want to hear about it and then next minute he does." And he sat smoking his pipe just as if he had no intentions of telling his story. Punk waited. Wasn't likely he *wouldn't* tell the tale since there was going to be a lesson in it for a certain boy.

"Got that pup on a trade," Hummy began, "and no sooner did I get him home than I saw I'd been hooked. Greediest dog it was ever my hard lock to own. Like to ate me out of house and home. It's a fact. Couldn't fill him up. That critter never thought there'd be another day or another pan of scraps."

Boy and man swapped glances. Wasn't any need for words. Punk was getting it all right.

"It was cram, cram, cram. Eat everything in sight he did. Gulp it up fast. Well, one day I went to look for him and I couldn't find hide nor hair of him, that is"—he paused and emptied his pipe against the heel of his shoe, " 'less you could call a little ole piece of stub tail, no bigger than the end of my pipe here, something."

"But what happened?"

"Well," the man cocked an eye at him, "the way I figger it, he crammed hisself so full, that he just blew sky-high like a log stuffed with dynamite."

"Really, Hummy, really?"

Hummy sort of shifted himself about. "Don't see anyone round here to gainsay it, do you now?" Then with his eyes twinkling he added, "Though I reckon it'd be danged hard to prove."

"But, Hummy—"

The man got to his feet. "There's one thing we're a-going to prove today, son, and that is just what sort of a marksman you calculate to be."

Punk immediately forgot all about the greedy pup and whether or not Hummy was making up the whole thing. He was going to shoot his grandpap's rifle! A cold shiver ran up his spine. Ever since Hummy had placed the gun

in his hand back at the cabin, he had been jumpy as an old woman about it. Maybe he wouldn't take to it the way his menfolks had. Maybe Granny had put the jinx on him with all her praying and talk about traipsing, hunting menfolks. Maybe. . . .

"Aim to peel the bark off that old elm twig at a hundred feet."

The boy's heart was in his mouth. Happen that *he*, Punk, would toe in at a hundred-foot mark and lift his grandpap's gun to his shoulder and peel that bark off quick as skinning a squirrel. Happen that he'd turn out to be the best marksman in the Ridgeland, outside of Hummy. Would a hard-headed granny woman take pride in that? . . . *Best shot in the countryside, Punk Bunn.* . . . It'd be talk all over the Rim. Like as not, it'd recall tales of his pap and grandpap who could outshoot anyone in the country.

*Ping!*

The elm twig ahead of him jumped crazily and then was still. Hummy had done exactly what he said he'd do. He'd peeled that limb as neat and easy as you please.

"Your turn, son."

The gun was in Punk's hand. He felt the heft of it, felt the smoothness of the stock. He was dazed for a bit. There he stood like a dunce with the gun in his hand, itching to use it but scared spitless he might miss. He lifted it to his shoulder.

"Can't aim with your eyes shut, son," Hummy said mildly.

Sure enough, Punk had squeezed his eyes tight shut. Of all the dumb things to do he reckoned that was the dumbest.

The despair and anxiety that had been riding him gave
over to anger at himself. With it came a cold determination
to succeed. He took a deep breath, aimed, and pulled down
on the trigger.

*Ping!* The twig limb jumped as skittish as a colt on a
frosty morn.

"B'jiggered!" Hummy gave a low whistle. "A natural,
Punk, a natural."

"A natural?"

"Plain born with a hawk-eye; no other way to say it,
a hawk-eye. Your pap and grandpap had it. Weren't nobody could outshoot 'em. Seen your grandpap many a time
toss a coin in the air and drill it, sometimes getting in as
many as four or five shots afore it hit the ground. And
your pap, he had a trick of barking the squirrel, he called
it. Ole squirrel'd be laying out on a limb and he'd aim for
the limb and with a single shot he'd have ole mister bush-
tail." Hummy shook his head remembering. "Them Bunns
were the shootingest, huntingest men in these here parts."

Punk stood straight and tall. Golly, he was sure lucky:
born with a hawk-eye. It was something to think about.
Hadn't been but a short time back he'd been thinking he
was the unluckiest guy anyplace and now look. It just
went to show how wrong a feller could be; how wrong
he could be about a lot of things.

"Been keeping that rifle till you was was old enough to
handle it, Punk. Reckon after today it's your own."

"My very own?"

"Yep. 'Course, it's been yours rightfully all the time,
it being your own grandpap's. But your granny couldn't
abide the sight of it, so I kept it till now."

Granny! Might have known he was flying too high.

What chance did he have to own a gun. Granny, feeling the way she did about everything, would be mule-minded on his having a gun.

"A feller has to stand up for his own rights, son," Hummy was talking real easy. "Not that I'd ever have you make a stand agin your granny, not agin Eliza Jane. But you're growing into a man and the gun is yours." He paused before going on. " 'Course, there's ways of making womenfolks see things in a different light."

"Such as?"

"Well—" The man took a deep breath as if plunging into cold creek water. "First, you got to show her that gun ain't goin' make no difference in doing your work and you don't aim to play hooky from school. Now and then you might sweeten her with a batch of fresh meat for her table—squirrels—nothing she relishes more than squirrels all stewed up with tomatoes and onions."

"One thing you better make up your mind to right now, son. If a man's worth his salt, he ought to wrap his kin woman right around his finger." Hummy squinted his eyes as if he were looking back through the years. Then he added glumly, "Reckon I come up short on that score."

"But Hummy, how does a man wrap a woman round his finger?"

"The onliest way is to sweet-talk 'em, son, sweet-talk 'em!"

Well, it was something to think about. Seemed as though he was as cram full of things as the greedy old pup and maybe he'd just blow sky-high and all they'd ever find of him would be a lock of red hair to prove it was Punk Bunn.

His laugh was giddy and gay. Hummy laughed too. And

it wasn't long before the hounds came loping over to join in on the ruckus.

Three days went by at Dynamite Gulch; days that overflowed into night, nights that ebbed into day. Punk marveled at the timelessness. Sunup, high noon, and sundown were the only time recorders out in the open.

Everything seemed to take on added significance. The sun, coming up over the hills, had the power to pierce through him and start his pulse up faster. The hum of the dragonfly that flitted past, or the whir of a grasshopper's wings, seemed to hold some special meaning. Even the fragrance of the air, the smell of sun on mint and clover, had the power to cut through him keen-edged.

When Hummy would take his noonday nap, the boy would slip down to the creek. He loved to sit quietly by the shallows, away from the main course of Clearfork. There he watched the world about him, held spellbound by the beauty and the wonder of it all. Butterflies winged themselves to the edge of the water. Wasps lingered in muddy spots. Small turtles lined themselves up on logs and sunned for hours. Once two wild canaries flew down to the water's brink, their wings opening and closing like fluttering moths. Indigo bluebirds came in numbers to bathe in rock ledges that cupped the water.

The wasps were fun to watch. They would set their wings and light on the surface of the water, letting the breeze skim them about as if they were tiny skiffs.

He confided all his findings to Hummy.

"You have the inner eye, like Mr. Robert Burns," his friend told him. "Someday you might put all these things down on paper. That is—you might, if you go to school long enough to learn how."

Right now Punk knew he was licked about going to school. If going to school could give a fellow the power to trap the glimmer of sunlight against the limestone ledges, to make crystal clear the moon coming up out of Clearfork, to catch the frogs bellow from the sand bars and the wind's sigh through the treetops with the whippoorwills a-calling, why then, a fellow wouldn't be wasting his time with schooling. Such a thing sure could change a boy's mind about school. It sure could.

There was no gainsaying what Hummy said, not ever. It was kind of spooky the way he could look down into a boy's heart; how he understood all about the choked up feelings that kept crowding around inside a body. Like now, knowing that Punk was wanting to do something about the things he'd seen and heard in the Gulch. He hadn't known what it was he wanted, he'd just felt himself to be all stewed up. Guess it was kind of like the yeast that kept working in Granny's bread dough, this mixed-up feeling that had been churning around in him.

Well, he wasn't so dumb but what he could see that he was changing his thinking about more than one thing. Seemed as though he was seeing everything in a different light. Maybe getting away from home had turned the trick or maybe just being with Hummy, who understood a boy's turn of mind. But whatever it was, he knew one thing for certain, he wasn't feeling sorry for himself any longer.

They were doing every single thing he'd ever hankered to do, from setting limb lines to hunting the coon hounds.

They had tramped through the timber, through the ravine, up and down hills, across sand bars, and waded the creek at least fifty times. They had back-tracked, they had circled; they had worked the living daylights out of the hounds.

Once they had gotten on the trail of Old Two-Toes. He'd given them a real workout just as if it had been a game of fox and geese. Tickled Punk to think how crafty and knowing the old coon was. He guessed he'd never forget the back-trailing and bewilderment of the hound dogs.

"Nary a dog on the Ridge a match for that feller," Hummy had said contentedly when the run was over and Old Two-Toes was still on his own.

He never had it so good. Consequently, it came as a complete surprise to Punk one night that he found himself thinking about the cabin on the Rim and the lone granny woman reading her Bible. Worrisome thoughts came to pester him like mosquitoes on a still evening. Happen she'd run out of stove kindling and had taken the ax to cut up more and the ax had slipped? Happen she'd climbed up on the roof to fix that old leak and had fallen and broken a leg?

It sort of took the edge off his appetite, this nagging feeling he began to carry about with him. Somehow Hummy's skillet biscuits didn't have the same flavor. It was worrisome. He kept seeing Granny's kitchen on bake day; the brown-crusted loaves of bread, the well-formed rolls, the fruit pies, or maybe a jam cake, all moist and spicy with filling and icing spilling out over the platter. It was a tormenting vision, after which he was unable to get back to his fine free thoughts of living out in the woods.

"Well, Punk?" The question roused him from a brooding spell.

"I got a feeling, Hummy. . . ."

"Such as?"

"Figure I'd best be getting along home."

Hummy nodded his head. "You've had your run, son." He grinned comfortably. "Reckon it's time to go home." And he began to whistle just as if it were the most reasonable thing in the world for a boy to want to go home.

But it was a fretting thing to Punk, past understanding.

## 6

# *Doing the Bristle Ridge Twist*

Punk finished the last mile at a steady lope. Wasn't any denying but what he'd learned a mighty good lesson from Hummy about the running fit. He'd just kept at a easy gait ever since he'd left Hummy and the dogs at Big Honey Creek and he was getting home in tiptop shape, not winded or sidetracked at all. Though he had to admit that his heart had jumped right up in his throat when he saw the roof of the cabin outlined against the sky.

"Granny," he hollered out, and letting go with all the speed he had, he pounded across the valley and raced through the door. "Granny, I'm home!"

He didn't have eyes for the wood stove that was cold, or the bed that wasn't slept in, he just had eyes for the granny woman sitting bolt upright in her rocking chair. At once, he knew something was wrong. Nighttime was for sitting down, not daytime, and here was Granny a-resting herself in the rocking chair just as if she were the easygoing Widder Gregg. But whatever her affliction was, it hadn't changed her way of speaking one whit.

"Land's sake! A body'd think I was deaf with all the hullabaloo you're making, young man."

"Granny, I'm home!"

"Humph. Got eyes in my head, haven't I? Reckon I can still see and hear even if I am getting along in years. Did you wipe your feet afore you came barging in here?"

"No'm." Punk just kept a-walking toward her.

Granny was more than a little surprised. "Reckon living in the woods makes a body forget his upbringing."

Punk was right beside her then and he bent down quick as a wind and kissed the soft cheek of his stepgranny. It gave him unexpected pleasure. But he was not prepared for the effect of his act on Granny. It was just as if the starch went out of her she so suddenly leaned back in the chair, closed her eyes and kind of wilted down. The boy saw then how peaked she was.

"Weak as a newborn kitten," she sniffed, brushing a tear from the corner of her eye. "Plain frazzled out with my suffering."

"Oh, Granny, are you hurt somewhere?" Punk's voice rose in anxiety.

"My land," she straightened in her chair and looked at the boy, "nothing to get your dander up, just pulled a muscle in my right arm and can't use it."

"When did it happen?"

"Last night."

Punk drew in his breath. Last night. Why, that was when he got the feeling he was needed at home. Well. It was something to think about. But right now he had too many things to do, first things first.

"You haven't had breakfast," he said accusingly.

"Been a mite queasy in my stomach," she answered.

"Nor slept in your bed last night." Punk's voice lodged another complaint.

"Had me a mind to sit it out, to wear out the pain so as to speak."

Punk went to work. He kindled up a fire in the stove, set the teakettle on to boil. He cut a slice of bread off the brown loaf and placed it to heat on the edge of the stove. He put the butter in a small pan to melt. He worked with quickness and sureness.

Granny sat and watched. "My soul on top of green earth," she marveled as Punk carefully rinsed out the old copper pot before setting the tea to steep. Her eyes followed his every movement in mounting disbelief.

"After we get some hot tea and some warm bread in you," Punk was saying, "we'll turpentine that arm. Might be a little bit of heat would draw out some of the pain."

"Might be," agreed Granny meekly.

"Of course," Punk went on, "if'n the arm don't get better, I'd best be getting ole Doc out to take a look at it. But the way I see it"—he paused as he reached high on the shelf for the bowl of sugar—"won't be no need of a doctor now that you got a man around the house to do the chores and rest you some and—well, take the load off your feet." The last was one of Granny's favorite expressions.

He brought the tea and the warm sugared bread to her on a wooden tray. "Now then, Granny, just sip this slowly and eat your bread. Soon as you get some food in your stomach chances are you'll feel some better."

"Chances are," yielded the woman weakly.

Punk was going right on with his orders. "It just might be more tasty if you dunked that bread into your tea so as it'd go down easy-like."

Granny's rocking chair suddenly came to life. "Young man," she said sharply, "I never did dunk my bread and I don't propose to start now, and if you'll get your thumb out of my sugar, I'll sweet my tea and get it down."

Punk laughed and pulled his thumb out of the sugar bowl, at the same time stepping on his granny's foot.

"Punk," she spoke very gently, "why don't you sit down and have a cup of tea, too? It might take the load off your feet." And as she said the last, the corners of her lips twitched and suddenly she laughed out loud, a happy, girlish laugh that swelled the boy's heart. "Land sake, off *your* feet!" and she laughed again.

Then Punk laughed and there were the two of them laughing together. It was a pure marvel, there was no other way to put it. To think the day would come when he, Punk, and his stepgranny would be sitting together drinking a cup of tea and laughing as cozy and comfortable as a mother hen and her chick in their nest. It made the boy feel warm all over and suddenly he was telling her everything about his stay in the woods with Hummy. His words came out, tumbling over one another in their eagerness to be said. He told all about Big Honey Creek and Hummy's cabin. And how the trumpet vine and the honeysuckle brought the hummingbird back each year. He told of Hummy's wild garden and how the toadstools and bits of green stuff with moss and button mushrooms ringed themselves about the old cottonwood.

He told of working the hound dogs and of the excitement of trailing Old Two-Toes. He recounted all his pleasures; of running through the timber, free and wild; of swinging from the grapevines and swimming naked in the creek water. It was a boy's world he described.

Granny was a good listener. She sat sipping her tea and keeping her black eyes on the boy's bright face, every now and then clacking with her tongue at some piece of information.

Punk halted himself right in the middle of a sentence. "B'jiggered," he said, sounding for all the world like Hummy, "I been running on and I haven't asked how you hurt your arm!"

"Varmint in the hen house." Granny's eyes snapped. "Heard all the commotion so I took me an ax and I went out and was whamming away with that plagued ax and I pulled a muscle, drat it! And the fox got away, too!"

"A fox!"

"Yes sirree. A fox! Faced me bold as brass, as much as to say, 'What right you get coming in here?' The red-tailed rascal! Killed twenty of my best pullets."

Punk was awed. It seemed as if Hummy's Old Man upstairs had a hand in this. Not that He wanted the fox to kill twenty of Granny's best pullets; no, not that. But He was paving the way for him to get that rifle in the house. There was no doubt about it. When Punk had come running into the cabin he'd left the rifle propped up outside against the wall. Now was the time to bring it in and make a stubborn granny woman see how impor-

tant it was for menfolks to own a gun. He stepped outside
the cabin and returned with the rifle.

"Reckon we'll be ready for that hen-stealing fox when
he comes back," he said.

He faced his stepgranny with the rifle held in his hand.
He held the gun in prideful ownership. His face shone
white and plain in his determination. He met the black-
eyed searching glance of the woman before him without
flinching.

"Where did you get that gun, Punk?"

"Hummy gave it to me. It belonged to my grandpap,
Billy Bunn, and it's rightfully mine, Hummy says."

"Hummy says! Seems to me it's been Hummy says this
and Hummy says that, ever since you come in this cabin.
What right he got setting himself up against what I have
to say?"

Punk was standing steady as a rock. He was a-going
to have his say, come what would.

"I know how to use the gun, too. Hummy showed me
how. And I reckon I'm a pert good shot. I peeled the bark
off an old elm twig at one hundred feet." He waited a
minute hoping to hear a word of praise from her. Receiv-
ing none, he went on doggedly. "Hummy says I'm born
with a hawk-eye. I'm a natural, he says; same as my grandpappy and my pap."

The woman let out a moan. "Oh, Punk, I don't want
you to be. Don't you see?"

"Reckon I do see, Granny. Hummy made it mighty
plain to me. He took me to Dynamite Gulch."

There was a startled cry from the woman.

"I'm beholden to him for the story, ma'm." Punk stood

straight and tall. "Worrisome things can be talked out
around a campfire. It comes to me that we're both better
off knowing we each know the story."

"Punk—" She tried to find words and failed.

It was the first time in all the boy's life that he had seen
his granny at a loss for words. Quick to take advantage
of it, he took his gun and walked to the fireplace. Carefully,
he lifted the rifle and laid it in the old rack above the
mantel.

Nary a word was forthcoming from Granny.

Remembering Hummy's story of the greedy pup, he
eased himself, careful-like, into the position of man of the
house: not being high-handed or pushy about any of it.

He swept the cabin. He dusted. He shook the braided
rugs. He was a whirlwind of activity while his granny sat
in her rocking chair and watched him.

He brought in the blooms of the chigger weed and the
stalks of the pokeberry plants and made bouquets for the
table. One night there was a bunch of pink milkweed
bloom beside Granny's bed.

"Weeds," sniffed Granny.

"A feller likes prettiness about him," Punk said then.
"And he favors color," he added, giving her black dress
a glance.

"Decoration is plain sinful," Granny stated.

"Who says so?" Punk questioned. "I just betcha the
Lord never figgered it so. He made all things, didn't He?
And from the beginning, He aimed on having things
pretty. It comes to me, if'n He'd wanted folks plain, He'd
never have done such a fool thing as making the earth
so plumb full of glory!"

"Punk. . . ."

But there was no stopping Punk. "He saw fit to decorate everything He made; why, even the commonest old weed has a bloom—and the scrawniest bush has berries."

She sat in silence. Punk waited anxiously, holding himself ready for a real fracas. After a spell of waiting, he saw Granny reach out and gently touch the flowers.

Then there was the business of Granny's hair. It had to be uncomfortable, sitting day in and day out with an uncombed head of hair.

One day she said, "Feel hamstrung. Can't do anything without my left hand. Awkward as all get-out having it in a sling. Reckon I'm going to need help with this pesky knot of hair."

She sat stiff as a hickory limb as Punk went to get her brush and comb.

"Always could get along by myself," she announced. "Many's the time I've fixed my own fence line."

Punk busied himself with her hair. He pulled the wire pins out of the tightly screwed-up knot that not even the three days of being unattended had loosened. Her hair spilled down her back, a mass of pepper-and-salt mixture. He took the brush, stroking until the sparks flew. And it was as if her hair came alive as he worked; the ends flying out and clinging to his hands.

He stepped in front and was brought to a dead halt. This was no stepgranny that he could recall. The woman sitting in the rocking chair, with her long hair hanging soft and warm and clinging, was a stranger to him.

"You, Punk!" Granny rapped out. "Get the slack out of your pants and get this plagued hair up and out of my way."

"Hummy says your hair was once black as the wing of a blackbird."

Her face pinked up and right away Punk could see that she was downright flustered, more like a girl than a stepgranny.

He figured he'd given her enough to mull over for the time being, and he went on about his work, parting the hair and beginning to braid one side. The hair made a handsome heavy plait.

He braided the other side, getting a little jumpy as he worked. Wasn't any denying what he was of a mind to do. He was plumb set on changing that tightly fisted knot into something more womanish. Hadn't he heard said that a woman's hair was her crowning glory? And a crown she was going to have. He folded the two plaits across her head, anchoring them securely with the wire pins.

"B'jiggered!" he gasped when he stepped around to look at his handiwork.

It was just as if he had framed a picture. The braids were soft and full, giving a gentleness to the face. Loosened bits of hair, fluffed out where once the hair had been skinned back.

"Pretty as a black-eyed daisy growing wild in the field," he began as Granny fixed her black eyes on him. "That's what Hummy said." He reached over for a flower, and taking it, he tucked it in back of her braid. Then he went for the small piece of looking glass and held it up before her.

Granny sat and gazed in silence. Twice she opened her mouth to speak. It was plain that some of her contrariness was missing.

"A feller takes pride in his kinwoman's looks," Punk said and then not able to hold himself in any longer, he broke out into Hummy's tune of the Bristle Ridge Twist:

*"Join your holts and circle to the left,*
*Break your holts and circle to the right. . . ."*

He was calling the dance just as Hummy had done and there in the kitchen before his stepgranny he began the steps that he had learned. Sashaying, circling, promenading right to the left, he fair lifted the pans on the stove with his rhythmic step. He was calling up the ghosts of the past as he whirled and strutted.

He saw that granny's foot was patting the floor in time to his calling. Was she remembering the Eliza Jane whirling in a red ruffled petticoat? Punk put all that he had in the tune and the dance, always keeping Granny in the center of things. He bowed to her, he circled her, he crossed the room, then back to her. He was raising such a racket that neither of them heard the door gently open, nor were they aware of the man who stood quietly watching.

Along about the last four lines, a deep voice suddenly took up the words. Punk didn't lose a step, he circled himself back of Granny's chair so that there was nothing between the man and the woman.

Hummy kept right on chanting the words as he matched them with a quick sure step and right over to Granny he promenaded and bowed. And the boy saw Granny get out of her chair, holding the bad arm careful-like in its sling. She curtsied deep. Oh, she was remembering the

Eliza Jane, all right. Punk knew such a lift of heart that he felt he fair might burst. Gently and easily, Hummy took her through the steps, calling the last lines. . . .

> *"Swing them by the elbow and back by the wrist,*
> *And don't forget the Bristle Ridge twist."*

They stood in the center of the kitchen, Hummy's arm about her waist.

"Howdy, Eliza Jane," he said softly, "welcome back."

Punk puzzled over that. Seemed as though his stepgranny should have said "welcome back" to Hummy, since Hummy was the one who had been gone.

## ✱ 7 ✱

# A Trip to the Ridge Store

Once a month, Punk and his stepgranny hitched the black horse, Gypsy, to the spring wagon and drove over Devil's Trail to the Ridge store.

Surely the kingdom above couldn't have any more likely treasures than the store's hoard. A boy could just stand and gaze and gaze and never get his fill of the plunder piled up on shelves, hanging from the walls and ceiling, stacked on the floor, and stored in barrels. How Mr. Huggins, the store owner, could know where everything was, completely balked him. He could lay his hand on any article asked for as quick and sure as a mouse could smell out cheese. Reckon he had eyes in the back of his head, too, the way he'd snort out at Toad Hood, "Let it lay, boy!" Or, "Mitts out of the pickle bar'l!"

There was nothing for free in that store, not by Mr. Huggins' will. But *Mrs.* Huggins, well, that was something different. Mrs. Huggins was a woman who had a hankering to fill up boys and girls, to take the chill off the

womenfolks who came a long way in the wagons, to
warm a man with a strong cup of coffee.

The gathering that congregated on store day was as
exciting to Punk as a fair meet. There were the regular
sitters. Wintertimes, they were lined up around the
stove; summertimes, they lounged out on the low porch.
The card players played their pitch game back in the
far corner. The traipsin' men—hunters, trappers, or fisher-
men—dropped in for warm-ups or a bait of food.

The womenfolks found their way over to the dress
counter to finger the bolts of dress material or exclaim
over prices; their high-pitched chatter rising over the
background of the men's steady rumble of yarns.

"Howdy, 'Liza Jane," Widder Gregg was the first one
to greet his stepgranny as they came into the store.

It was plain bad luck, running headfirst into Widder
Gregg: not that Punk could see anything quarrelsome
about her, nor could the other menfolks who loafed in
the store. They found her company might pleasuring,
calling out to her and joshing with her. But that always
seemed to rile Granny more. He guessed the maddest he'd
ever seen Granny was the time Hummy was in the store
and he and the widder got to cutting up.

Granny tried to tie up the hard feeling with the sausage
grinder that the widder had borrowed and had claimed
as her own. But a boy'd have to be plumb dumb not to
see the way Granny bristled and hackled up whenever
Hummy mentioned Widder Gregg.

"Mighty sorry to hear about that arm, 'Liza," Widder
Gregg's voice was sweet as molasses.

"Mended now," snapped out Granny, vinegar sharp.

"Heard tell you was out in the hen house after a fox."

"One time you heard right."

"Ladies"—the gentle voice of Mrs. Huggins couldn't have sounded any better to Punk than Melly's voice on the trail—"I've a mind to show you some new merchandise I've been keeping under the counter till a passel of you womenfolks showed up."

Punk shook his head over womenfolks. One minute they could be facing one another like two wood cats, and the next second they'd be flocking together like pullets in a hen house. He sure had to hand it to Mrs. Huggins, though. She'd not only eased things down, but most likely she'd be making some sales by the sound of the oohs and ahs coming from the five Ridge women, who were crowded about the counter.

His curiosity whetted, the boy moved in closer and took a look for himself. Mrs. Huggins had put five new hats on the counter; hats that were sure prettied up with bows of ribbon and wreaths of flowers. They'd be Sunday-go-to-meeting hats for 'most everyone there, 'cepting his stepgranny. They'd be hats bought to pleasure their menfolks.

He cast a quick look at his granny and saw her pick up a pert little hat with a yellow velvet ribbon and a red rose nestled on the brim. She was turning it slowly in her hand when Corrie Belle Gregg reached out, hawk-fingered, and lifted it quickly to her head.

"Red and yellow, catch a feller," Corrie Belle sang out, capering herself out into the middle of the floor, drawing the men's eyes to her as naturally as bees to honey. She was rosy and plump and the hat was mighty fetching on top of her loosely waved hair.

"I reckon a hat like that would sure be good bait on any mantrap," drawled a familiar voice. And there was Hummy.

Granny turned her back. "Leave tomfoolery and self-gratification to the foolish," she rapped out. "And if there's anyone in this store'd like to fill out my order, I'd be obliged."

As Mr. Huggins bustled up, Punk caught a kind of hungering look in his granny's eyes. It kind of did something to him. He couldn't rid himself of the riling in his stomach even when Hummy's hand dropped to his shoulder and drew him into the circle of men lounging close by.

"This here boy is sure cut from the same cloth as his grandpappy," said Hummy. "With a little more practice and there'll be nary a one of you to outshoot him."

The response from the men was gratifying and Punk's dejection lifted as he found himself seated in the midst of them, listening to their talk.

"There's a whopper of a big acorn crop coming up," one of the Snow brothers brought out. "And there's more coon tracks along the creek than you can shake a stick at."

"Old Two-Toes sure has been having himself a time," put in Gum Muller. "Been showing himself bold as brass in broad daylight!"

This was the kind of man talk that Punk loved the best. He hugged his knees tight up against his chest and tried to keep his excitement cooled down.

"Coming home from frogging just at sun-break the other morning, and I run smack dab into him! Face to face on Devil's Trail!"

The men stirred and expressed their amazement.

"What happened?" Punk couldn't stand the suspense.

"Well, sir, the trail's narrow and it was me and him,

face to face; each wanting to go our way, but neither one of us wanting to step off for the other fellow." He shook his head recalling exactly how it had been. Then he laughed kind of sheepishly and confessed, "Dog take it, if that cuss didn't outbluff me."

The men hooted.

"For a fact. He just kept coming on toward me, slow and gritty, with a wicked gleam in his eye as if he was a-spoilin' for a good fight. And me without nary a club in my hand."

"Had me a coon once straddle my neck," confessed Hummy. "Got the scars yet."

"Sure," Gum nodded vigorously, "and I plain didn't want to tangle with anyone like Old-timer!"

"So?" urged Punk, wanting to get it all told at once.

"So," drawled out Gum, keeping his eyes on Punk's excited face, "I jes' plain stepped off the path, out into a hunk of poison ivy, and I takes off my cap and I bows low to Old-timer and I says, 'Yore Majesty,' says I, 'pass on by.' An' that Ole Two-Toes looked me over mighty careful, then he kind of drew back his lips in a grin and moseyed on down the trail."

The men hollered and slapped their knees in appreciation.

"Always been saying I'd like to bag Old-timer, all of us has said it one time or another, but shucks. . . ."

Hummy nodded. "Reckon the day he's caught, there won't be no fun trailin' again."

"But Toad and Spider, they're out to get him," burst out Punk. "They been setting traps all summer!"

Dark looks came over the men's faces. There wasn't a one of the men there that didn't respect sportsmanship and a fair deal.

"Some day," predicted Hummy, "the Hood brothers will get their comeuppance!"

"But how? When? Who'll give it to them?" Punk demanded.

Hummy looked at the boy for a second. "Well," he said reflectively, "only the Old Man upstairs knows the how and the when. It's anyone's guess as to who it'll be. But it'll all come about one day, and it just might be that you'll be the one."

"Me?" Punk's voice rose high.

For quite a spell, he sat without saying a word. The men went on with their talk but Punk wasn't listening. He was too occupied with the terrible picture of himself being chosen to give the Hood boys their comeuppance. The thin, ornery face of Toad projected itself so clearly in his mind that he could almost feel his sour breath in his face. Added to that was the thought of Spider and his spooky dumbness. All in all, it was a scary notion.

"Punk." His stepgranny's voice reached him.

He shook himself free of the specter of the Hood brothers and went over to her.

"My soul on top of green earth," she scolded. "Sitting around with them traipsin' men as if we had all day. Now get a move on you and tote these sacks out to the wagon. Seems like everyone around here is bent on wasting time."

Punk carried some things out to the wagon and came back in for another load. Bending down to pick up a large burlap sack, he backed into the counter where the pert new hat had been left by the Widder Gregg, knocking it to the floor.

Granny was quicker than Punk in stooping and picking up the hat. She held it for a second, studying it carefully.

"Widder Gregg sure looked mighty pretty in that hat," Punk prodded in a lowered voice.

Granny dropped the hat on the counter. "Pretty is as pretty does," she said. But the usual conviction of tone was missing. And Punk saw that she looked plumb fagged out.

"While I'm about loading the wagon, Granny, seems as though it might be neighborly for you to have some of that spiced tea I smell coming from the back room."

And even as he said it, Mrs. Huggins appeared and had her usual say, "Step in for whiles, Eliza Jane. I've finished the quilt, the birds-in-the-air pattern, remember? And it'd pleasure me to show it to you."

Granny gave a few minutes consideration to the invitation; then as was the usual procedure, she nodded her head.

She turned to Punk as Mrs. Huggins went ahead.

"If a boy's old enough to sit around with traipsing men," she muttered for Punk's ears only, "then I reckon he ought to have spending money in his pants pocket."

Punk stood rooted to the floor as his stepgranny whisked through the doorway into the back room. Loose change was now tightly clutched in his fist where his granny had poked it.

Cracky. Cautiously opening his hand, he found fifty-five cents. He was mighty thankful he was wearing his everyday pants with a pocket where he could keep his change. He pushed his hand down into the pocket, spreading his fingers and letting the change free to jingle there.

He wandered over to the glass jars with the candy: the jelly beans and the licorice sticks; then to the glass counter with the fancier pieces of candy, the cocoanut candy made into strips of bacon and into the American flag. He feasted his eyes on all of it.

Moving reluctantly along, he came to the hardware counter, where the knives, the leather thongs, and the shells for his gun were kept. Even though he studied each article, all the while he knew what he was going to do with his money. And after he made the entire tour of the store, he came back to the counter where the new hats were.

"Mr. Huggins," he gulped, being careful his voice wouldn't reach out to the men. "I'd like to buy that hat." And he pointed to the one with the yellow velvet ribbon and the red rose on the brim.

Mr. Huggins peered over his glasses. "Got you a girl, son?"

Punk reddened and shifted about uneasily. "Well, I guess—that is . . . well, maybe I have."

"Got to see the color of your money, son. Can't do business without money, you know. This here store aims to treat all the customers the same. It's cash on the barrel head."

Punk dug down in his pocket, bringing up his change, and laid it on the counter.

Mr. Huggins made a big thing out of counting it; making much of the pennies until finally he reached the sum of fifty-five cents.

"You'll have to dig deeper, boy," he rumbled. "Not giving hats away this season. That there hat will cost you a round dollar."

"A dollar!" Punk was set back. A dollar was hard come by on the Ridge, all right. He calculated that cutting fence posts might be a way of earning a whole dollar. But it'd take time to line up such work, and in all likelihood the hat would be gone.

"Forty-five cents more, boy. If sums are the same now as when I went to school, forty-five plus fifty-five makes a dollar!" Mr. Huggins droned out for all the world like the auctioneer at the Saturday sales.

Punk began to feel nervous. He plain didn't know how to deal with a man of Mr. Huggins' caliber, but one thing he did know, he had to have that hat.

Seemed like that prettied-up hat had become so all-fired important to him that he couldn't turn back now. Wasn't no way to put into words the way he felt about that beribboned, flowered hat. For a fact, he *had* to have it, the same way he had to have his grandpappy's gun.

A man could look downright foolish dickering over such a thing as a head gear for his womenfolks. But a stubbornness settled in on Punk and he squared himself to make a stand.

"Reckon the forty-five cents'll have to wait, Mr. Huggins," he said, rocking back on his heels the way he'd seen Hummy do when he was driving a hard bargain.

"Wait?" The storekeeper's eyebrows shot up in amazement. "See here, Punk Bunn, word's been getting around you're gettin' mighty biggity. Since when does a leggy young 'un tell a store owner his money can wait?"

"When he shows a store owner that by waiting, forty-five cents just might grow into right smart more."

Mr. Huggins sucked on his teeth a moment and gave some consideration to the idea.

"What'd you have in mind?"

Punk kept his voice steady. "Come wintertime, I'm set to go trapping."

"Humph." Mrs. Huggins' eyes narrowed as he sized up his quarry. "You mean you and me'd split fifty-fifty on skins you'd tote in here?"

Punk's eyes widened.

"You want me and you to go pardners, Mr. Huggins?
You furnish the shells and the traps and me forage round
and bring in the game?"

"*Me* furnish the shells and traps?" Mr. Huggins' voice
rose.

Punk could hardly keep his face straight. "Cracky, Mr.
Huggins, that's a good offer, but I'll have to take it up with
my friend, Hummy, over there. You see he's mighty strict
about business deals and—"

"Now see here, boy." Mr. Huggins' face was turkey
red and he was having trouble keeping his voice down.
"Ain't no need in bringing Hummy into any deals twixt
you and me being as how I ain't figgering on any fifty-
fifty split. Jes my way of having my fun, you know."

He took his handkerchief out of his pocket and mopped
at his bald head. "As a matter of fact, that there hat is
yours right now with the understanding my forty-five cents
is a-coming to me when you sell your first batch of skins."

Punk hoped he was keeping his glee down deep.

"Plus ten per cent," the storekeeper rapped out, "for
carrying you on my books, you understand."

"Five!" Punk countered swiftly, rolling his eyes in the
direction of the men in the corner.

"A deal," hastily conceded Mr. Huggins, shoving the
hat down into a brown paper sack with one hand and
raking in the change with his other hand.

Punk walked sedately out to the wagon and carefully
stored his parcel back under the wagon seat. He was fair
dizzified by his luck. He'd made a trade with old man
Huggins. What's more, he'd held his own and there weren't
none who'd say he'd been took. His pent-up feelings boiled
and churned in such a mixture of elation, triumph, and

rejoicing that he threw back his head and let out a wild whoop.

In a second, he was joined by Melly and Old Red, who had been lazying in the shadow of a large white oak at the side of the store. Both dogs and the boy hit the ground in a tangle of legs and hound dog tails. Rolling and wrestling, the dogs uttering growls as if they had a varmint, they finally ended up at the store door.

"I declare!"

Lying on his back with the dogs clambering all over him, Punk looked up and saw his stepgranny and Hummy watching. Hummy wore a broad grin on his face, but Granny had a set look to her mouth.

"Get right up from there, Punk Bunn!" she ordered.

Punk rolled to his feet, holding Melly and Red away from him.

"Now look at yourself!" Granny sounded real cross. "Dirt all over that clean shirt."

"Well, now, 'Liza, it'll all come out in the wash," Hummy drawled easy-like.

He gave Punk a quick wink as he added, "B'jiggered. You standing there hollering about his shirt puts me in mind of my old granny."

'Liza Jane turned on Hummy in a flash. "Your old granny! Well, Hummy Humphreys, let me tell you there's twenty years difference twixt your old granny's age and mine!

Granny, mad all the way through, climbed into the wagon seat, her black eyes shooting off sparks.

"Climb up in this wagon, Punk," Granny ordered. "We're going home."

She startled Gypsy with a loud slap of the reins on

her back and they took off down the road, lurching and showering dust from the wheels.

They drove along at a rapid pace, neither one saying a word. Gypsy, being part Morgan, could reach out and fair eat up the road. It was a delight to watch her pick up and set down her feet. But Punk didn't feel the usual exhilaration. He was downright glum. Like as not, there'd be a feud on now twixt his granny and Hummy and there'd be no more pleasuring evenings by the fireside, or trips down to the cottonwood cabin. He was feeling sorrier and sorrier for himself, when suddenly he was nudged in the ribs.

"Here," his granny said. And he found the reins pushed into his hands, the reins that drove Gypsy! And Granny never allowed anyone to drive her black horse.

But he didn't have time to think about the oddness of female critters as he was settling down to driving. Managing Gypsy took a bit of doing. She was plenty high-spirited and could cut up something fierce if she'd a mind to. All kinds of things could happen and it was a chunk of responsibility. Horses could shy, or they could run away. They could step in a hole and break their leg. Sometimes, in fording a creek, buggies had been turned over.

Down the road, they drove, Punk keeping his eyes on the road and on his horse. They rattled across the bridge, they made the sharp turn at the black oak, they forded Big Honey Creek. Granny never once gave out instructions or nagged at him. A good feeling of companionship warmed him.

They slowed down and were kind of ambling along when they came in sight of the Hood house. Punk had been so taken up with his driving that he had overlooked the fact they were taking the old road home. This route he usually avoided as it ran right past the Hoods' place.

He sighted anxiously on each side of the road, remembeing that Ma Hood was at the Ridge store *without* her boys. 'Course, there was every chance Toad and Spider were out in the woods worrying some poor critter. Still, it was always wise to keep one's eyes peeled for any kind of meanness.

Gypsy saw them first. Her ears pricked up and she kind of took little mincing steps the way she did when something spooked her. And right at the edge of the road, sitting in waist-deep grass, were Toad and his slinking dog, Judd. He couldn't spot Spider right off; Spider, like most wild animals, felt safer in the trees. No doubt he was on some overhanging limb near his brother.

Having Granny with him was some consolation, that is if a boy took any pride in hiding behind a petticoat. But pride and the Hood boys couldn't be used in the same thought, the Hoods not having any of it themselves.

He sat up straight, holding the reins carefully. Toad was scrambling to his feet, plain gawking at the sight of Punk driving the black mare.

Punk couldn't help gloating at the way Gypsy was high stepping it off. Reckon he was handling her mighty well, too.

Toad stood with his mouth hanging slack. Punk knew what he was thinking, all right; ole Bunny Rabbit was driving Gypsy! Well, ole Bunny Rabbit was doing a good job of it, too.

Punk tried to keep his face straight but the sight of Toad

looking as if his wits had been addled was more than he could handle. It made him feel bold and reckless.

As they drove on by, Punk turned and stuck his tongue out at Toad.

He got action then all right. A clod of dirt struck the back of the wagon, startling up Gypsy into a swerve that nearly unsettled the two in the wagon. Punk had his hands full. Gypsy was tearing out, putting a quick distance between them and the boy in the road. But even so, the harsh voice of Toad Hood rose and reached them as they were passing over the hilltop.

"Yah! Yah!" he yelled. "Ole nanny-goat! Ole nanny-goat! In 'er black petticoat! Wears a crazy bonnet with no trimmin' on it!"

Granny's hand reached over and patted Punk's knee.

"No need to get your dander up, Punk."

Tears of rage filled his eyes and threatened to spill out. He tried to keep his face turned from Granny's look.

"Nanny-goat—nanny-goat—nanny-goat . . ." trailed faintly away behind them.

Granny smoothed down her black petticoat and then reached up and straightened the black bonnet.

"A nanny-goat," she said thoughtfully. "Well, it begins to look as if I been as hard-headed as one."

Not another word was spoken on the way home.

# 8

# *At Coon Rock*

The day Punk was to give the Hood boys their comeuppance was a day like any other August day on the Ridge.
The sun came up bright and hot, shining all day, and then
setting in the west, in a red ball of fire.

"Reckon I'll leg it over to Horseshoe Lake for a swim,"
he announced when his last chore was done.

"Be back afore dark, Punk," his stepgranny said, adding
gently, "Dusk time is a lonesome time in a cabin when
its menfolks are away."

Punk flashed a swift smile at her. Then he was out of
the cabin and his feet were fair skimming the earth as he
took to his heels. Light of foot and light of heart, he raced
down the hill into the shade of the woods.

Slowing down, he took a deep breath. No matter how
often he came to the woods, he was always taken with
the mystery and the quiet. Reckon some day after he'd

131

had his schooling, he might get it all down in writing for
other folks to read.

It came to him that he'd felt mighty sorry for himself
the early part of the summer. He recalled the lonely feeling that had pestered him so. Well, for a fellow who had
thought he had scanty fare, he sure had ended up with
a big bait.

Yes sirree, reckon now things were of a different cloth
with Granny eased down. Soon he'd be able to tell her
about the hat that was hidden up in the loft. He drew
a deep breath, savoring the idea, thinking just how he'd go
about it. He was glad he hadn't been like Hummy's greedy
pup and blown everything sky-high by pushing.

With so much to think about, it was no time at all until
he was in sight of Coon Rock and Horseshoe Lake. He
paused on the crest of the sloping hill to take a long look
at the place. There was the huge boulder that was Coon
Rock, reaching up into the meadow and wild hay field.
There was the waterfall spreading over the rock, filling
the lake with foam. Bet there wasn't any place in the world
quite so pleasuring as this spot. He pure relished the idea
that he was part of the land. How had Hummy put it?

". . . there are some who are born to the land. And no
matter where they roam, or how far a piece they travel,
there's one place that will call them back. . . ."

And this was the place. Maybe it was written in the
chapters of his life, he didn't know. Reckon he was too
young to be giving thoughts to such. But the thoughts all
unbidden rose up in him at times and fair took his breath
away.

Questions churned up in him but he could find no answers. Was it possible for anyone ever to know all the whys and the wherefores that plagued a fellow?

He might never know the answers. But he knew he'd be puzzling about them as long as he had life in him. Cracky, but it was all a funny world. Grownups made as many mistakes as young 'uns did. Well, it was too much for a boy to think about, especially when Horseshoe Lake was there ahead of him, waiting to receive him for a cooling off.

He began pulling off his shirt and then his pants, being careful to roll them up and hide them in the crotch of the oak tree by him. Being prepared was mighty important in the woods. One never knew what might slip up on him. Hummy had pointed out more than once that in pioneer days the way they had survived was by keeping a keen lookout at all times.

"No matter how peaceful a place be, a smart fellow always gives it a scance; that is, if he wants to be all in one piece. How else do you reckon did Daniel Boone make it through these forests? He looked afore he stepped, let me tell you." Those had been Hummy's very words.

Punk grinned to himself as he recalled them. Well, he'd look afore *he* stepped, too. So he gave a long look to his surroundings, taking in the countryside. Then he brought his eyes back to the waterfall. Reckon the heavy fall of rain had made it so dark. In dry spells, the water trickled pale and sickish. But now it glowed in shades of mint green, flowing and spilling down the slope in darker shades.

He couldn't wait any longer to feel the cool water on himself. He was right ready to jump forward when, suddenly, he was aware there was someone else in the woods besides himself. The crackling of underbrush and snapping twigs grew into more definite sounds of pounding feet.

Punk sat very still and listened. He could tell that whoever it was, was heading for Horseshoe Lake. Then the sounds ceased for a second only to be revived in a few seconds by a loud shout.

"We had him, Spider! We had that ole son-of-a-gun! We sure did!"

It was Toad Hood's voice that rose in the timber: as ugly a sound to Punk as the caws of a thieving crow robbing a bird's nest.

"Look a-hyar, Spider! Old Two-Toes done had the trap sprung on him. Brung the blood, b'golly! *Wh-o-o-op-ee!*"

The sweat on Punk's body seemed to freeze so that a chill settled in on him. He clenched his teeth and wished desperately he had someone to turn to, man-size and real like Hummy.

"Hyeaah! Thinks hisself smart, huh, gittin' away. Well, he done run smack into his doom. Looky at them bloody tracks. We got that rip-tailed scooter, sure as sows drop litters! Hyar! Hyar's the trail and it's leadin' us right whar that old bandit done holed up!"

Such fury rose in Punk as to leave him sour-stomached. Old Two-Toes, king of Clearfork and of Big Honey Creek, the smartest coon on the Ridge, tricked by the meanness of the Hood boys. It couldn't be.

"Old Two-Toes is the spirit of the wilderness," Hummy had said. "He's all the fine, careless, free things . . . he's Nature pitted against man and his gun and his hunting dog."

Punk's mind raced. Could the fine free things survive in the world without help? Hummy had said most men hankered for life to be fine, though it wasn't an easy thing to come by; and sooner or later, a fellow must make a stand. Did he, Punk, have to pit his measly strength against Toad Hood who went bear hunting with a switch? Say now, was this the time for the comeuppance that Hummy was talking about?

Punk groaned, recollecting the last beating he'd had from Toad. If only he had someone with him. But it was as Hummy had said. A time came in a fellow's life when he had to stand on his own feet, alone, defending what he thought was right. Guess it was time.

Punk Bunn stood up. He pushed aside the shielding oak leaves, making his presence known; not with a blast of trumpets, nor a great handclapping, but with a manly dignity he was unaware of.

"Hey!" It was a single word. It had no distinction to it, but in all likelihood it was one of the bravest words Punk Bunn was ever to speak.

Toad and Spider were startled into a dead stop. They had been carefully tracing the tracks of the crippled coon along the sandy ledge of the lake to the side of Coon Rock.

Punk walked down the slope towards the Hood boys, each step bringing him closer to the mean-featured Toad and the dumb boy, Spider.

Toad was the first to speak.

"B'jig, jig, jiggered! Hyar's my meat for supper!"

Spider's feet played a swift, happy shuffle on the ground.

"Bunny rabbit meat, ain't nuthin' tastier, is thar now, Spider," Toad said with a leer.

Punk kept right on walking toward Toad, easy-like, considering what tactics to use. Bluff was his only weapon,

he knew right well. He could never hope to win in a physi-
cal combat, but maybe there'd be a chance at using the
brain God had given him. The thing was to act quick and
put Toad on the defensive.

"Setting traps out of season again, Toad Hood!" he
began. "Reckon if the hunting men at the Ridge store
heard about this, there'd be a considerable amount of hard
feelings, riled up feeling."

Toad stood stock still and thought, his eyes peering
craftily out over red rims.

"Take Hummy Humphreys for instance, and the Snow
brothers, and Gum Muller, too," Punk was talking calmly.
"Fair play's mighty important to them. I'd sure want to
sidestep a-past any of them if I'd been caught trapping out
of season."

"A tattletale, b'jig!" Toad spat tobacco juice right at
Punk's feet. "Wal, the way we handle them kind ain't
fitten fer them fair-play men to watch."

"Toad," Punk was steady as a rock, "I don't aim on
tattling. Seems as if you and me could strike a bargain.
Let Old Two-Toes go; let him hole up where he will and
we'll call it quits."

"Quits? Huh! You and me? We ain't never quits till I
t'ar your innards out with my bare hands!"

"It seems to me, Toad, you livin' in the woods and all,
you'd understand about Old Two-Toes. He's a part of
the Ridge same as Horseshoe Lake, the creek banks, the
big timbers—why, same as you and me."

"Wal, now ain't that purty! Did you hear that, Spider?
As purty a spiel as I done ever heared!" Toad's lips were
peeled off his gums. "Teacher talk goin' round, you maybe

gonna be a writin' guy some day. So's I figger hyar and now, it be up to Toad Hood to give you somethin' to put down in yore book."

Toad's big hand reached out and clamped itself about Punk's neck.

"Don't be twistin' round, bunny rabbit. Ain't no way fer you to get out of this 'un."

The smell that rankled Punk was as unpleasant as that of a wet dog. He was toe to toe, shoulder to shoulder with Toad Hood, a hulking brute of a half-grown man, who never had *right* on his side, but who, forever and a day, seemed to need only his *might*. What chance did a scrawny boy like Punk Bunn have, a boy who had been brought up by a stepgranny who preached, " 'Do unto others as you would have others do unto you.' "

"Hyeah, Spider! You watchin'? This hyar gonna be plumb comical! I aims to put a considerable dent in ole bunny rabbit's head! You watchin'?"

There were no answering foot taps. Punk felt Toad's hand loosen around his throat as he turned to look.

At the same instant, they both saw Spider, who had left the bank and was crawling up the narrow path on Coon Rock.

"Hyeah! Spider! What you up to?" yelled Toad.

Spider turned, waving jubilantly back to his brother. With his left hand, he pointed back behind him to the coon tracks and then in front of himself. He was perched precariously close to the waterfall.

"Consarn it!" Toad ran down a piece. "Git off'n that slick rock! You want to drown yourself?"

The dumb boy grinned and hunched himself flat against

the wall of the rock, inching himself along. It was plain
he was trailing the crippled coon straight to his hideout.

Punk stood rooted to the spot. Was his secret of Coon
Rock to be discovered? He was bogged down with dread
as the thought came to him, that Old Two-Toes had taken
himself to the secret cave under the waterfall. It was bound
to be. Crippled from the trap, he'd known he'd have to find
refuge close by. By all the signs of the bloody tracks, he'd
made it to the cave, his last stronghold. Maybe he wasn't
so badly done in but time and rest would heal him; that
is, if he could keep hidden for a spell. And now, there
was Spider not far from the hanging moss and spilling water
that screened the small opening in the rock.

"Come on, Spider." Toad's voice was a whine of fear.
"Come on down hyar!"

It came to Punk right out of the blue that Toad was not
only deadly afraid of the water, but he was half out of
his mind at what could happen to his brother. He cared!
Toad Hood cared about something besides himself! It was
almost beyond believing. Cracky, here was one of those
lessons that Hummy could have told him: even the mean-
est human beings had feelings.

"Spider, whatcha want to do that fer? Git down, I say!"

It happened then. Spider's foot hit against a slimy piece
of moss and he started slipping there before their eyes,
his hands wildly snatching at rock and moss. Toad and
Punk stood rooted to the place for a second.

Toad plain went crazy. He let out a howl like Judd
gave when kicked in the ribs and began running up and
down the bank. Punk knew, as did everyone on the Ridge,
of the Hoods' fear of water.

His heart leaped right up in his throat and nearly choked him. He'd seen a drowning boy once when the Big Honey Creek had overflowed. It had been a sight to haunt him in many a nightmare: the wildly clutching hands, the frantic churning of the water, and then the terrible stillness.

He was lonely and frightened as he realized there would be no help coming for Spider unless he, himself, was the rescuer. And being a rescuer didn't mean he could save Spider or himself, either. B'dogged, if he owed the Hood boys anything! Why should he risk himself for this miserable dumb clod who had plagued and tormented him as long as he could remember? Why?

Spider's head bobbed up out of the water; not a sound coming from his open mouth, his white hands despairingly churning the emptiness. Another wild howl came from Toad, who was now ankle-deep in water, as if he'd throw himself into the lake. His terror was past bearing.

Punk dove into the water, cutting the surface cleanly and surely. He surfaced and sent his body hurtling through the water. Didn't seem as if he'd had any other choice being raised as he had been by a "do good" stepgranny.

He reached the spot where Spider had last gone down and tread water, being careful to keep a distance. He knew he'd be no match for the dumb boy's frightened strength should he get within arm's reach.

Again, Spider's head bobbed up, his eyes as wild and terrified as any trapped animal in the woods. He saw Punk there almost within reach and a look of hope flashed into his eyes, jolting into Punk like a slug in his innards.

He waited anxiously for the boy to come up again, measuring the exact time he could swim in safely. As Spider came up the third time, Punk came in from the back, putting an arm lock around Spider's neck, lifting the dumb boy's face out of the water. There was no fight left in Spider. Punk was able to pull him in to the bank where Toad was quick to haul him up on dry land.

All in the world Punk wanted to do then was to lie down on the bank, catch his breath, and think about things. But the ruckus Toad was making with his blubbering and calling out to Spider made it clear to Punk he wasn't through. He was plumb frazzled out, but that didn't mean he was going to get any rest. He pushed Toad out of the way as he bent over Spider and went to work, pumping out the water in the boy's lungs by the methods Hummy had taught him.

"Dead! Dead! Dead!" howled Toad.

"Oh, pipe down!" Punk was real cross. As far as he was concerned, it'd been better if Nature had made Toad dumb, too. "He's only water-logged!"

He rolled Spider back over just as his eyes opened. Punk found himself looking directly into Spider's eyes, eyes that met his in a long, knowing look. Punk marveled at the expression. Cracky, that dumb Spider was sharp as a needle. He watched as Spider's eyes looked up at Toad, then out at Horseshoe Lake, up to Coon Rock, and back to Punk. It was plain his mind was sorting out each fact and putting everything together.

Toad flopped down on his knees and grabbed Spider up in a bear hug.

"I'm gonna bash yore head in, Spider, you do sumthin' like that again, you hyar?" The two boys looked at one another a moment, then Toad said, "Aw, Spider, I thought you was dead!" And he rocked him back and forth in his arms, comforting himself.

Punk wondered if he'd ever understand anything. Because the Hoods were bullies and ornery, he'd never thought about them having feelings. He grinned suddenly to himself. He was learning, he reckoned. Guess it'd take all of a lifetime to learn the things he wanted to know.

Spider was suddenly at his side, looking directly into his eyes. He had something to say. Punk watched as Spider first tapped himself on the chest, then he reached out and touched Punk's shoulder. His touch was light as a moth settling on a stalk. Wasn't anything scary or upsetting about it, the way Punk had always figured it'd be. But then his figuring didn't seem to be adding up. Like now, would he ever have thought that Spider Hood, the dumb boy of the Ridge, would be talking to him? Or that they would understand one another?

Wasn't any chance of *not* understanding the smile that was on Spider's face as he clasped each of his hands together in a handshake. It was a bid for friendship. Punk nodded his head. Seemed as if Spider was all stewed up with longing to show his gratitude. Abruptly, the boy whirled about and bent down, picking up the steel trap that had been sprung by Old Two-Toes. He lifted it and dangled it there for Punk to see and then in a wide, arched movement, he swung the trap far out into Horseshoe Lake.

Toad let out a howl.

"Whatcha doin', Spider? You lost yore mind? You gone crazy, huh?" And the hand that only a few minutes before had been gently patting his brother, flayed out and gave him a cuff on the side of the head.

Spider reached down for a rock and advanced.

"Now, Spider, now. . . ." Toad began backing away.

Spider gestured to his brother and then to Punk. With a sweeping motion of his arm, he took in all of Horseshoe Lake and Coon Rock at the same time, shaking his head at Toad.

"No sirreee!" bristled Toad. "I ain't gonna promise that! I ain't gonna say we don't set traps along hyar no more. Reckon we 'uns got as much right to this hyar spot as that ole bunny rabbit thyar. . . ."

Spider let go with a well-aimed rock, at the same instant bending and picking up another one.

"Aw, come on, Spider," Toad whined, "don't be a-startin' that. If'n that's the way you want it, all right. But jes' wait till Ma hears about you throwin' away a good trap. Jes you wait. . . ."

Spider gave Punk a quick, knowing look, again clasped his hands together and then turned in the direction of home.

"I'm much obliged to you, Spider," called out Punk, glorying in the reformation of the Hood boys. Guess his feelings were like Brother Trapp's when he led his flock in the paths of righteousness . . . guess. *Wham!* Toad, passing by, delivered a hard kick to Punk's shin, then he was gone on a dead run. For a second, Punk was so clabbered up with hard feelings that all his lofty thoughts flickered out.

He rubbed his shin, feeling kind of foolish. Well, a leopard didn't change its spots after all. Things had been happening too fast and he'd been kind of muddled, but now he was back on familiar ground.

It began to seem funny. He laughed. He laughed at him-

self, at all the cuckoo things in the world. His laughter
stirred the woods back of him. A whippoorwill called out
its evening plaint, a saddened cry for all mankind. An
owl let out a harsh hoot, a hoot of derision as if men were
too absurd to be taken seriously. And Punk laughed again.

He was all fired up with being a growing boy with all
the time in the world ahead. He raced along the bank and
jackknifed into the water. He held his breath and dove
to the bottom of the lake. He came up and filled his lungs
with air. Turning over on his back, he floated free and
easy as a leaf, ending up at Coon Rock. Face up, under
the trickling water, his eyes blurred until the green of
moss and fern, of light and shadow, blended into streamers
of color.

He felt himself suspended in a crystal bubble, and for a
moment it was as if he saw the whole world and all the
people in it. All the answers were there that had plagued
him for so long. Punk was filled with light and warmth,
and a great knowing grew in him; until suddenly the
crystal bubble shattered and he was just Punk Bunn not
knowing really *what* he knew.

He turned and swam to shore. He shook the water
drops off himself and slowly started up the narrow path
of Coon Rock. He'd have a look in on Old Two-Toes now,
that is if he were hiding in the cave.

Pausing at the spilling waterfall, he looked about. All was
easeful. Quickly, he ducked under the water, sliding himself through the narrow opening in the rock.

The darkness of the cave blinded him. He waited for
his eyes to adjust to the murkiness.

A rustling, a stirring close by set his pulse to throbbing.

It was plain spooky. What if it weren't Old Two-Toes; what if it were something else? A wildcat, say?

Careful-like, Punk began to move back to the ledge where he kept his candle stubs and matches. His fingers fumbled for endless seconds before they hit upon the deerskin-wrapped parcel.

Remembering to take his time, easy-like he lighted the candle. Didn't know when light had been more welcome. He held it cautiously out and up and had himself a look around. There! He caught his breath. There not more than two feet from him was Old Two-Toes, all hunched into a large ball with his sharp, bright eyes fixed on him.

Punk spoke softly, "Hi, Old-timer."

Boy and coon looked at one another. The coon's eyes caught the glint of light and seemed to throw off sparks. Punk knew a big boar coon that was cornered could be mighty mean.

"Are you all right, feller?" he questioned, keeping his voice low. And then he scolded, "How come you walk right into a trap, as old as you are and as smart as you are? How come?"

As if reassured by Punk's voice, Old Two-Toes accepted his presence in the cave and began to lick his paw. The boy saw it was the right one and that it was bloody. He sighed. Guess they were lucky at that. A coon'd know how to take care of an injured foot and licking it was the best medicine in the world.

"What business you got getting so careless? Tell me that! You ought to have your head examined!" Punk's voice rose.

Old Two-Toes paused and looked over at the boy as if his words had registered.

He kind of ducked his head as if in agreement and then his mouth pulled back for all the world like a grin. Punk felt good all over. Old Two-Toes was going to be all right.

Blowing out his candle, he placed it back in its wrappings and laid it onto the ledge. Then he slipped out of the cave.

The trickle of water eased off his shoulders, down his back, as he sidestepped out from under onto the edge. He looked down into the swirling water of the lake, watching the foam float lazily on the surface. Punk felt good as he dove deep into the clear, cool water.

## 9

# *The Bright Road Ahead*

Dawn comes up on a Sabbath day in much the same way as on a week day. But to Punk Bunn, the sun that came up on this particular Sabbath was as unlike any sun he had ever seen. It was as if there were a splendor to it, a special, shining kind of light.

He took the hat from its wrappings, the hat with its velvet ribbons and its flowers, and he held it up happily. Cracky, but it was pretty, like the wild primroses that grew in the fence rows. And it was just what he wanted for his stepgranny, for Eliza Jane, the frolicking slip of a girl who could outdance anyone on the Ridge—the girl who had worn a red ruffled petticoat under her full skirts.

Punk stood stock-still, recollecting how he'd made inquiry as to *that*. Right out of the blue, he'd asked her, "What happened to your red ruffled petticoat?"

Granny wasn't one to show amazement but she'd stiffened

straight as a ramrod, puckered her lips together, then right crossly had demanded, "Land's sake, whoever told you about that?"

"Hummy."

She'd looked kind of flustered and downright surprised. "That man! Think of remembering anything so foolish."

The rocking chair had been stilled and then Granny had walked over to the wooden chest that had stood alongside the fireplace as long as Punk could recollect. She'd opened it, gone right down to the bottom, pulling out a red ruffled petticoat! She'd given it a shake so that there was a crackle and a snap. The color had been as bright as a red-headed woodpecker.

"I been a-keeping it all this time," she'd admitted.

"Well, it's pretty enough to keep," he'd said careless-like, "though of course, 'tain't likely you'll ever be wearing it."

Granny had eyed him sharply. It'd been hard to keep back the laugh that had bubbled up in him.

It was then he had asked her, "How come you put away your red ruffled petticoat and all the things that were pleasure-giving and lively?"

She'd looked at him then, not angry at all, acknowledging him as a grownup. Her words were chosen as carefully as the eggs she selected for her setting hens.

"Well, now, son, it's just as Hummy said, there was a bitterness in my soul. I was willful and stubborn and I wanted to humble myself.

"A punishment?"

"Maybe."

She'd sighed and as quick as a flash, she'd bent down and kissed him.

"A nanny-goat, Punk, a hard-headed nanny-goat all these years!"

And they both laughed long and loud the way people do who have been close to tears and heartbreak.

Punk shook the thoughts away from him and, holding the hat carefully, he went down the ladder into the room below.

" 'Liza Jane," he called out softly, keeping his hands with their gift behind his back.

An astounded granny woman whirled about to face him.

" 'Liza Jane, is it! You're covering ground mighty fast, Punk Bunn. Plain mannish now! What happened to that skinny, shirttailed boy who plagued me to death with willfulness and sulks?"

"I reckon the same thing happened to him as did to that stubborn stepgranny who was forever and a day pestering a boy to pieces."

The two looked at each other in contentment.

"Here." Quickly, before he thought better of his act, the boy held up the hat for her.

Granny stood rock-still, only her eyes moving to look long at the hat, then fixing themselves on the boy's face.

"Your spending money?"

"Yes'm," he gulped and then plunged on, "and some pelts to boot come winter time."

Apprehension built up in him. The stepgranny he'd once known would have poured words of wrath down on his head, but now it made him a trifle skittish the way she looked so frazzled out.

Her hand reached out and touched the hat, fingered the velvet ribbon, and brushed the petals of the flowers.

She was soft-spoken as she said, "You set a heap of store by prettiness, Punk."

"I reckon so. But it's not vanity, Granny. It's just that pretty things make a person forget the mean, ornery things."

"Sakes!" Granny said.

"Granny, it'd pleasure me for you to wear this hat." There. It was said.

Granny was as gentle as a mourning dove when she gave answer.

"Our church folks call a hat like this an adornment. Reckon you know that, Punk."

"*Nature* adorns everything!"

"Church folks and nature don't be the same things."

"Is there anyplace in the Bible that says you can't wear a pretty hat? Is it a Bible rule? Is it?"

Granny studied a moment. "No, I'd say it were plain out a man-made rule."

As soon as she said it, her mind was made up. Wasn't any gainsaying, she'd be censured by the elders; but the women would understand. Hadn't they talked among themselves about there being no verse in the Bible specifying women had to be everlastingly dressed in black.

"A man-made rule," she repeated firmly, not foreseeing that the spark kindled in her heart was the first step toward freeing the women of the church from their somber attire.

"There." Punk hoped he didn't sound triumphant.

But he was saved by the sounds of baying hounds and there at the doorway was Hummy, close crowded by Red and Melly, who were pushing to get at Punk. Hummy heeled off the dogs and sent them padding along to the shade of the water oak. The man had other things on his mind 'sides dogs and a boy. Even Punk could see that.

Why, Hummy was as slicked up as a peeled elm sprout. His thick, graying hair was brushed back and his tanned face was razor clean. He was wearing a blue shirt, starched and ironed.

The grin that tugged at his mouth was puzzling to Punk. It was a kind of mischievous grin as if he meant to stir up trouble.

"Mighty pretty hat you got there, 'Liza," he drawled out. "Aiming to wear it to prayer meeting?"

Punk caught his breath. It was a dare, a plain out and out dare, the way he said it.

Eliza Jane threw up her head just like Gypsy when a rabbit bolted out under her feet. The cabin crackled with unsaid things. Somehow, the boy knew it was more than just the hat that was at stake now. Guess his granny knew, too. She turned the hat kind of gentle-like in her hand, keeping her eyes on Hummy's face as if he were a stranger.

Punk shook his head. Would there ever be a time when he could right out understand what grownups had in mind? He'd learned many things during the months, but dogged if he could figure out what was going on twixt these two.

"Go out and harness up Gypsy, Punk." As sweetly as the wooddove's call, came Granny's voice.

Punk, spellbound, gazed at his once contrary, hard-headed granny who had raised him. She looked the way a fellow always longed for his womenfolk to look. It wasn't just the braided hair that had changed her. It was something inside.

But things were still mighty skittish. Punk saw her

mouth tighten as she took in Hummy's appearance. It was the freshly starched and ironed blue shirt that held her eyes.

"Too much starch in your shirt, Hummy Humphreys!" she snapped out.

Hummy winked at the boy. Wasn't anyone could turn out a better shirt than Widder Gregg when she was of a mind to and when she was in need of some spending money for some new frippery.

Granny whisked around the corner and disappeared into the back room. Punk went out, hitched up Gypsy, then he was back in the cabin. He walked over to the basin, wet his comb, and slicked down his hair. He began feeling kind of nervous. It looked as if he had cooked up a mess of powerful victuals. He wished he could be as calm as Hummy. Hummy was waiting as peaceful as if he were on the creek bank, his lips puckered, whistling a tune.

Cracky, but waiting was an uneasy thing. It was the not knowing part that got a fellow all frazzled out. This big wanting had been with him all summer. Seemed as though all the paths they had taken, the three of them, had been leading just to this.

There was a quick step into the kitchen; Hummy broke off his whistling, Punk turned to look. The new hat in all its beflowered prettiness was on Eliza Jane's head. And it looked as a hat should look on a pretty woman's head. But neither Hummy nor Punk said a word, the look in Eliza's eyes not being the kind to allow any liberties at the moment.

She walked over and picked up the Bible. There was a swishing sound as when the cottonwood leaves bent to a breeze.

"You, Punk!" She startled the boy. "Is Gypsy ready?"

"Yes'm."

"Hair combed? Hands washed?"

He nodded.

She turned without another word then and marched out to the wagon with Hummy and Punk close on her heels. Punk untied Gypsy and leaped into the seat. Hummy was standing alongside of Eliza on the ground as if he were going to help her into the wagon.

"And where do you think you're going?" snapped out the woman, tilting her head so that the flowers on the hat kind of quivered.

"To see the fireworks," answered Hummy as calm as anything. And without a by-your-leave, he picked her up and deposited her in the center of the seat.

It was all done quickly, but not so fast that there hadn't been a sudden flash of color and the hem of a red ruffled petticoat for a second caught on the wheel. Disentangled, it disappeared under the black overskirt.

Punk caught his breath and waited for Hummy to say something. But without a single remark, Hummy sprang in to sit beside Eliza Jane, landing light in the wagon.

Gypsy immediately sensing the turmoil of those in the seat back of her, was off in a flurry, skittish as a colt. Punk tried to ease her up and keep his hands light on the reins. He kept thinking one of the grownups would reach for the reins. But he might as well have been alone for any help coming from *that* direction.

It was a heady feeling going to prayer meeting with folks he was proud to claim. He let Gypsy have her head and they were fair eating up the road when they came within view of the Hood house.

Punk kind of drew up on the reins. He couldn't help

but wonder what to expect when he went by; that was
if the Hood boys were home. He hadn't seen either of
them since the day of the near drowning. But it would be
a pleasure to show off his stepgranny in her new hat;
especially to ole Toad, who had taunted and name-called
so many times in the past.

As he neared the house, he began looking on each side
of the road. The Hood boys were as secretive as the wild
animals. Well he knew their habits of hiding in tall weeds
or up a thickset branch or behind a tree trunk. And only
when Gypsy began blowing and puffing out her nostrils,
was he made conscious of the fact the boys were there.

They were now traveling at a walk. Neither Hummy nor
Eliza Jane was saying a word.

There was a thud. Gypsy sidestepped and had to be
pulled up tight. There in the road in front of them was
Spider. He had dropped off a low hanging limb and was
holding up his hand. Punk tried to appear nonchalant as
if this were the usual run-of-the-mill happening. And then
Spider made the same gesture he'd made at Horseshoe Lake,
hands clasped together in everlasting friendship.

Punk waved at him and said, "Hi, Spider." He couldn't
help wondering how his granny and Hummy would take
it, they being aware of how the Hoods had treated him all
during the years.

But it was plain it wasn't Spider that his granny was
interested in. She was looking at Toad Hood, who was
standing in the tall grass, his ugly mouth all agape. He was
right ready to yell out his rhyme at her, the way he had
for as many Sundays back as Punk could recall. But the
sight of the woman with the velvet-ribboned, flowered hat

on her head, sitting so easy-like, shushed him. There was also the fact that the greatest hunter of the woods, Hummy Humphreys, was seated in the wagon, too. He stood muddle-headed.

Punk was right ready to drive on when he felt a movement beside him. The first thing he knew, there was his stepgranny standing up in the wagon, standing up and looking directly at Toad Hood.

Cracky, what was she up to? Why, she was doing a chant, a chant just like the hateful one that Toad had spat at them for over the years. But the words were different.

> "Old Granny Bunn wears a hat with a rose . . .
>     and with velvety bows!
> And the old nanny-goat wears a red ruffled
>     petticoat!"

Before either of the two male occupants of the spring wagon knew what she was about, Eliza Jane pulled up her black skirts daintily, ankle-high. She was showing off the red ruffled petticoat.

Punk and Hummy sat as still as Toad stood. Then Eliza, with a pleased look on her face, sat down amidst a swishing of skirts and said, "Drive on, Punk."

The boy stole a look at her as they set off down the road. He saw her eyes all squinted up and her lips held tightly together to keep back the laughter. He tried to hold himself in, but couldn't. Then it was too much for all three, and the wagon rocked with mirth.

And as easily as that, Punk felt his arm linked by his granny's and saw her other one with Hummy's.

His heart soared. He was with his own folks, and though neither was blood kin, he reckoned they'd been tried by fire and were bound to him forever. And suddenly, he felt fine and free, the way Old Two-Toes was. Just being alive, just being Punk Bunn with all the years of living ahead was pure satisfying.

The hounds, Melly and Old Red, padded contentedly alongside the wagon; the wheels turned easy in the track.

Sunlight blazed out, sparking sand and limestone, and the road stretched ahead full of light, a promise of the future.